"Cassie." *He* stood there.

She blinked, waiting for the image to vanish.

Instead, one brow cocked up and he tipped his cowboy hat back on his head, the morning sun shining on his face.

She blinked again, harder. He didn't move. He didn't waver or vanish. He stood there, all too real. "Sterling?"

"Yeah." The voice rolled over her, deep and gruff and so familiar her throat went dry.

Sterling... She couldn't breathe or think or look away. It might not make sense for him to be here now, but he was. Just as big and strong and handsome as ever. It wasn't fair, really. He had no right to stand there, looking like he belonged, while those warm brown eyes swept over her face.

He wasn't surprised or rattled or the least bit... upset.

She swallowed. Why should he? He was the one who left. He wasn't the one left behind.

She resisted the urge to slap his face or run away. The past was the past and she was so over it.

Right. Sure. Keep telling yourself that.

Dear Reader,

Happy holidays and welcome back to Granite Falls!

Cassie Lafferty has appeared on the page many times throughout the Texas Cowboys & K-9s series—now it's her turn to find love and happiness. It's Christmas in Granite Falls and Cassie is settling in to enjoy her favorite time of year... Until Sterling Ford, the man who broke her heart, arrives in town.

When Snowmageddon hits, Sterling rescues her—and the box of abandoned puppies she was taking home to nurse. Sparks fly when they reconnect over these cuties and old wounds turn into new possibilities. I hope you enjoy your stay in Granite Falls and that you have a wonderful holiday season.

All the very best and see you next time you're in Granite Falls!

Sasha Summers

A Snowbound Christmas Cowboy

SASHA SUMMERS

HARLEQUIN
SPECIAL
EDITION

**HARLEQUIN®
SPECIAL
EDITION™**

Recycling programs
for this product may
not exist in your area.

ISBN-13: 978-1-335-72430-4

A Snowbound Christmas Cowboy

Copyright © 2022 by Sasha Best

All rights reserved. No part of this book may be used or reproduced in
any manner whatsoever without written permission except in the case of
brief quotations embodied in critical articles and reviews.

This is a work of fiction. Names, characters, places and incidents
are either the product of the author's imagination or are used fictitiously.
Any resemblance to actual persons, living or dead, businesses,
companies, events or locales is entirely coincidental.

For questions and comments about the quality of this book,
please contact us at CustomerService@Harlequin.com.

Harlequin Enterprises ULC
22 Adelaide St. West, 41st Floor
Toronto, Ontario M5H 4E3, Canada
www.Harlequin.com

Printed in U.S.A.

Sasha Summers grew up surrounded by books. Her passions have always been storytelling, romance and travel—passions she's used to write more than twenty romance novels and novellas. Now a bestselling and award-winning author, Sasha continues to fall a little in love with each hero she writes. From easy-on-the-eyes cowboys and sexy alpha-male werewolves to heroes of truly mythic proportions, she believes that everyone should have their happily-ever-after—in fiction and real life.

Sasha lives in the suburbs of the Texas Hill Country with her amazing family. She looks forward to hearing from fans and hopes you'll visit her online: on Facebook at sashasummersauthor, on Twitter, @sashawrites, or email her at sashasummersauthor@gmail.com.

Books by Sasha Summers

Harlequin Special Edition

Texas Cowboys & K-9s

The Rancher's Forever Family
Their Rancher Protector
The Rancher's Baby Surprise
The Rancher's Full House

Harlequin Heartwarming

The Cowboys of Garrison, Texas

The Rebel Cowboy's Baby
The Wrong Cowboy
To Trust a Cowboy

Visit the Author Profile page
at Harlequin.com for more titles.

Dedicated to all the real-life heroes out there:
on the front line and on the homefront

Chapter One

Cassie Lafferty was a woman on a mission. *Coffee*. After that, she'd be ready to face the day. She gripped the handle of the dual leash as the dogs led her down Main Street. They knew where they were going—no matter the weather—it was their morning routine. But she couldn't remember the last time she'd made the trek bundled up in her faux-fur-lined wool peacoat, her feet warm and toasty, encased in thick socks and her bright tangerine-colored rain boots.

"It's cold, isn't it, boys?" She always talked to her dogs—and she knew full well that they listened. Bert, her mixed, shelter pup who resembled a giant coppery-orange carpet, and Ernie, her sleek black-and-white Labrador mix, trotted along with their tongues lolling and their tails wagging. Neither seemed the least bothered by the sudden drop in temperature. "I bet it'll clear off and be sixty by noon." She smiled as Bert looked back at her, giving her a doggy grin.

To say there was a chill in the air was an understatement. It was below freezing—something that happened a few days at most in Texas. But, according to the local news stations, there was a winter storm coming through. Gusting winds, rain, snow *and* ice… That was unusual in and of itself. But before Christmas? That was unheard of. Most cold snaps happened in late January or February—if one happened at all.

"Hey, Cassie." Dean Hodges stopped wrapping colored Christmas lights around the old-fashioned lamp post in front of his shop. It was up to the shopkeepers to decorate "their" streetlamps—making downtown alive with color and holiday spirit. "You ready for the storm?" He reached inside the front door of his store, Main Street Antiques & Resale Shop, for the treats he kept on hand for any canine visitors. "They're saying it's going to be a hundred-year storm."

"I guess I'm as ready as I'll ever be." Cassie had wrapped the pipes of her small house, made sure she had batteries for her flashlights and camping lanterns, chopped wood for her wood-burning stove and had plenty of food and water for her and the dogs. It helped that she was an avid camper—in a situation like this, her camping supplies came in handy.

"Good. Glad to hear it." Dean opened the plastic container full of dog treats.

"I'm sure they're saying thank-you for the treats." She laughed, watching her dogs sit, ears perked up and tails wagging in unison.

"I think you're right." Dean offered them both a dog biscuit. "It's not like they've been getting treats from me every morning for the last, oh, six or so years." He gave Ernie a pat and scratched Bert behind his floppy, shaggy ear. "I guess you could say I'm reliable."

Cassie nodded. "And they appreciate it." She hoped he'd leave it at that. Dean was a good guy—a really good guy, according to her brother—but he wasn't the one for her. No matter how sweet and handsome and *reliable* he might be, she didn't see Dean *that way*. Dean, however, hadn't been discouraged when she'd said as much. In fact, he'd said she was worth waiting for. "Come on, boys. Momma hasn't had her coffee yet."

Dean stepped back. "I'd classify that as an emergency." He waved them on. "Get your Momma her coffee, boys." He gave her a wink and went back to wrapping the streetlamp.

Cassie gave him a little wave, thankful he'd kept things light, and continued to The Coffee Shop. Part of her wished she could give Dean a chance. He was a good guy. An honest, kind, hard-working man who was thought highly of—by all. After her last relationship, with Mike, she should be thrilled to have a good guy. Her relationship history was short and a *good guy* hadn't figured into either of her heartbreaks. Dean would never break her heart.

But the other part of her wanted...*more*. It didn't help that everyone around her had their happy ending. Like flowers and poems and *all* the romance. From her brother, Buzz, to her brothers-by-choice, the Mitchells, all of them were contentedly wrapped up in their own blissful love stories. It was wonderful and, at times, absolutely unbearable.

"At least I have you two." Cassie glanced down at her dogs trotting happily along the sidewalk. Synchronized wagging. It was a thing. At least, it was for Bert and Ernie. Sure, Bert's tail was all fluff and Ernie's was a more streamlined rudder, but that didn't matter. Wag for wag, their tails kept time and pace. "You'll love me forever, won't you?"

Bert and Ernie both looked back at her.

"I love you, too." She smiled, shivering against a gust of icy northern wind. "And, yes, I'll see if Reggie has any extra bacon for you." Regina Hernandez, Reggie to most everyone, owned and operated The Coffee Shop. The shop had only been open a couple of months, but it was always crowded. Not only did Reggie make the most amazing pastries Cassie had ever tasted, she offered a variety of coffee—all freshly ground. Plus, she normally had a little something set aside for Bert and Ernie, which meant they were almost as excited as she was to reach the painted-glass front door.

"Morning." Reggie waved from behind the glass cabinet. "Morning, boys." She waved at the dogs. "Alonzo, can you get this gentleman taken care of?" She left her teenage employee to handle the man at the counter and headed Cassie's way. "New lipstick?"

Cassie shrugged as she unwrapped the long blue scarf she'd knitted last year from around her neck. "I felt colorful this morning." Cassie didn't have a makeup drawer, she had a lipstick drawer. Lipstick was pretty and fun and easy to change up. "Sugar plum." She puckered her lips for show. "Seasonally appropriate name."

"I like it." Reggie nodded. "I could never pull off a plum shade."

"I'm not sure I am either." Cassie shrugged. "But I'm wearing it anyway. Are we still on for tonight?"

"I'm so excited." Reggie's sarcasm was playful.

"I know, I know. Not exactly what you pictured yourself doing on a Saturday night?" Cassie shrugged. "Welcome to small town living."

"You keep saying that." Reggie grinned. "Actually, I think it will be fun. I'll bring some cookies, too. For tonight and tomorrow."

"They will love that. And I appreciate the help." Not only had Cassie roped Reggie into helping her with bingo at the community center that evening, she'd signed Reggie up to volunteer for the Christmas Light Festival and Parade. Every year, Granite Falls had thousands of visitors come to town to take pictures beneath the lights wrapped around the giant oak trees surrounding the courthouse, with its clock-tower steeple. It was a big deal, a very big deal, and a perfect way for Reggie to meet folks and make connections.

"What about the storm?" Reggie asked.

"I don't think it'll be as bad as they're predicting but I'll let you know if something changes for tonight." If a winter storm really hit Granite Falls, bingo would be cancelled. But tomorrow's planning meeting? "I can't imagine the Christmas Light Festival and Parade planning being postponed—ever. It's barely a month until Christmas, after all. But I guess we'll find out." They only had one week until the lights came on, not a lot of time to get a whole lot done. Not that Cassie minded. She loved Christmas. She loved Granite Falls at Christmastime. *Besides, what else am I going to do on a Saturday night?*

"If the storm hits and bingo gets cancelled, you can come to my place and watch that British show with all the baking. They have a holiday special." Reggie sighed, tucking a curl behind her ear. "Yeah, I know, my Saturday plans are sort of pathetic."

"At least we're in this together." Cassie laughed, determined to put an upbeat spin on her lacking social life. It's not like she didn't have options— er, an option. Dean would step up if she gave him even the slightest encouragement. Considering how immediate her response was to the idea of encouraging Dean, there was *no* way she could *actually* encourage him. Besides, he was a good guy. He deserved a woman that would appreciate him.

After chatting through the evening's logistics, Cassie ordered a peppermint coffee, a delectable looking gingerbread pastry, a bacon and cheese roll for the dogs and said her goodbyes.

"Good mornin', Cassie-o-mine." Angus McCarrick held the door open for her. Once she was outside, he swept off his hat, the outrageous flirt.

She smiled, adjusting her hold on the leash. "Morning, Angus. Dougal."

"Cassie." Dougal, Angus's twin, touched the brim of his hat, his gaze shifting beyond Angus. "Um…" He elbowed Dougal hard, nodding in the direction he was looking. "You headed to work, Cassie?"

Angus's eyes narrowed, a furrow creasing his brow. "Damn," he murmured under his breath.

Cassie nodded, glancing between the brothers. "Yes…just for a few hours." She started to turn, but Angus sidestepped and blocked her view.

"How about you come have coffee with us first?" Angus asked. "Tell us how things are going at the clinic—that sort of thing."

"That sort of thing?" Cassie almost laughed. "Why do I get the feeling you're up to something? Oh, right, because I've known you two forever and I know when you're up to something." She shook her head. "Bert, Ernie, say goodbye to Angus and Dougal." She lowered her voice, and growled, "Goodbye, Angus and Dougal." She waved, stepped around Angus to head back down the sidewalk, only to come to a screeching halt several steps later.

"Cassie." *He* stood there.

She blinked, waiting for the image to vanish.

Instead, one eyebrow cocked up and he tipped his black felt cowboy hat back on his head, his cheeks red from the snap in the morning air.

She blinked again, harder. He didn't move. He didn't waver or vanish. He stood there, handsome and big and all too real. He was *here*. In person. "Sterling?"

"Yeah." The voice rolled over her, deep and gruff and so familiar her throat went dry.

Sterling... She couldn't breathe. Her brain seemed to lock up. But her gaze stayed glued to him. Processing. After all these years... It wasn't fair, really. He had no right to stand there, looking like he belonged and as gorgeous as ever, while those warm brown eyes moved slowly over her face.

He wasn't surprised or rattled or the least bit... upset.

She swallowed. *Why should he be?* He was the one who'd left her. She remembered how easily he'd walked away, his hate-filled words and unfounded accusations ringing in her ears. She had been left behind with no explanation for his sudden and total change of heart. After he'd gone, she'd wasted her days struggling to make sense of it all—to think and breathe and go on, now that the future she and Sterling had hoped and dreamed of together no longer existed. *So many wasted days.*

From the corner of her eye, she saw the look Angus and Dougal exchanged—concerned and wary, all at once. Right. This was awkward for everyone. Her and Sterling's breakup hadn't exactly been private or civil. Friendships had been challenged and lines had been drawn.

She wished she could pull some scathing set-down out of thin air instead of standing here, shocked into silence. The urge to slap his face or run away or vomit on his toes were vying for top spot—but then, she'd give him a reaction. She didn't want to give him anything, especially her dignity. *Been there, done that.* The past was the past and she was so over it. *Right. Sure. Keep telling yourself that.*

"Bert?" His voice rumbled on as he crouched, smiling at the dogs. "Ernie?" The mingled surprise and tenderness in his voice made her chest tight.

Stop staring at him. Acting like the perfectly normal and completely unaffected person she was shouldn't be all that hard. But that meant not ogling how muscled his jean-encased thighs were, how his khaki weather-all jacket was taut across the breadth of his shoulders or how big and strong his leather glove–encased hands were. She blinked, tearing her gaze from him.

The McCarrick brothers were no help. Angus, with his arms crossed over his chest, and Dougal, his hands shoved in to his pockets, were both having a hard time making eye contact with her. Almost guilty. Had they known he was coming? Is that what that look meant?

"Last time I saw you two, you were puppies," Sterling said, oblivious.

Which stirred up a tenderhearted memory Cassie would be wise to ignore. *In and out.* Slowly. *Stay calm.* Once she got to the clinic, she could hyperventilate all she wanted to—with no one around.

"You're both huge. Bert, with all that hair, you look more like a bear than a dog." Sterling chuckled, scratching Bert behind the ears. "You're not as shaggy but just as big." He patted Ernie. Then he stood and turned to face her.

She focused on the painted coffee-cup sign over the door behind him, not the man standing beneath it. Yes, this was better. *I can do this.* Time had passed. People moved on and she and Sterling, well, they were strangers now.

"Y'all have a good day." She waved, her pastry bag slipping from her fingers.

Bert perked up, tugging against the leash for the bag, but Sterling moved too quickly. He caught it and offered it to her.

"Thank you." She took the bag, careful not to touch him. "Okay." Walking away. Eyes forward, not looking back... So far, so good.

By the time she'd walked to the other end of Main Street, the Granite Falls Veterinary Clinic & Animal Hospital lights were on and her brother's truck was parked out front. She clutched her now-squished bag to her chest as she backed through the front door, led the dogs inside and took a deep, wavering breath as the door closed behind her.

"Hey, Cassie." Skylar Mitchell looked up from the computer. "I'm loving this cold weather. I know we were all in shorts last weekend, but I had to put the girls in sweaters and honest-to-goodness coats this morning. They looked *so* cute."

Cassie nodded. "It's nice." She pushed off the door and turned, staring out on to the street for any sign of... No one. She swallowed, stepping back.

"What's up? Who are we looking for?" Skylar asked, coming around the counter to stand beside her. "What are you holding?"

Cassie glanced down at the squished bag. "Oh. A snack, for the boys." Her gaze darted down the street to the coffee shop. No Angus. No Dougal. No Sterling. The need to hyperventilate was easing.

"Cassie?" Skylar's hand rested on her shoulder. "What's wrong?"

She tore her gaze from the coffee shop and Main Street and turned to find Skylar, Bert and Ernie all staring at her. "Nothing." She forced a smile. "Well, my gingerbread pastry is now mashed into a sausage roll, but that's about it."

"Okay." Skylar didn't look convinced.

"I'll get right to work on the books." When she

wasn't grooming the animals of Granite Falls next door, she handled the accounts for her brother's veterinary clinic. Today, a screen full of numbers might just be the thing to steady her nerves. And the sooner she was done with work, the faster she could head home and get things together for tonight's bingo and tomorrow's meeting. Everything would be fine. She'd stay busy, the cold would fade by midday, and Sterling Ford would leave and he'd go back to being her biggest heartbreak, nothing more.

Sterling sat at one of the wooden café tables inside the coffee shop, numb. Christmas carols played from the speakers overhead, the distinct scents of ginger and peppermint filled the air, but inside—*nothing*. It was for the best. Feeling nothing was better than feeling…everything.

He turned his coffee cup, his gaze sweeping the shop. The place hadn't been here last time he was in this neck of the woods. The cutesy chalkboard signs and fancy aesthetic weren't his thing, but the coffee was good and he was seriously considering buying two more sausage rolls—even if he'd already devoured three. Other than the coffee shop, things looked pretty much the same as they had when he'd been in town three years ago. Three years. The last time he'd come to town to talk to Cassie—and left with a broken nose and an ass kicking. It'd been a short, but unforgettable, trip. Sometimes, it felt like a blink of an eye, other times, near a lifetime ago.

He kept turning the cup between his hands, doing his damndest not to look out the picture window, down the street—again. He'd known full well he'd see Cassie while he was here. Hell, he hadn't planned on leaving Granite Falls until he'd seen her. He'd been hauled out of town before he'd talked to her last time. He'd be damned if he left before sitting down and talking to her. Not bumping into her on Main Street, though. He hadn't been prepared for that—or her.

"You weren't expected for a few days yet." Dougal studied him over his coffee cup. "You could have called."

"I like showing up unannounced. I get to see the real thing—not the cleaned-up, ready-to-deal version. Besides, contract negotiations side, I wasn't sure what sort of reception I'd get." He sipped his coffee, a slight edge to his voice. He'd put the McCarrick brothers in a sticky situation and they weren't happy about it. "Considering last time we saw each other."

"When you had a bloody lip?" Angus asked, looking a little too smug for Sterling's liking.

"And your eye was near swollen shut?" Sterling quipped back.

"Here we go." Dougal shook his head and finished his coffee. "If I recall correctly, you were both bleeding and hurt when I stepped in between you two." He set his empty coffee cup on the table. "There were no winners that day."

But there had been a loser. Sterling stood and threw his and Dougal's empty cups into the trash can—his gaze immediately drawn outside until he found it. Granite Falls Veterinary Clinic & Animal Hospital's green awning was barely visible from where he stood. He'd been left a little too rattled for comfort by their brief encounter.

Cassie, beautiful as ever, had stared up at him with big eyes and as good a poker face as he'd ever seen. That was new. His Cassie had always been so easy to read. He'd loved that. One look in her eyes and he'd known what she was thinking—or near enough, anyway.

This morning? He had no idea what she was thinking or feeling when she'd seen him. And it left his stomach in knots.

"Taking in the view?" Dougal was giving him serious side-eye, throwing more trash away. "Not much has changed in Granite Falls, Sterling."

"No?" Sterling asked, taking his seat at the table. "Figured I'd see for myself."

"How long are you planning on sticking around?" Angus asked.

"Why do I get the feeling you're not all that happy to see me? You two aren't much of a welcome wagon. Guess escorting folk out of town is your preference?" It was a dig and they all knew it. Did it feel good to lord a little power over them? Yes. His smile was tight. "I'm happy to take this contract elsewhere. This is purely business for me."

Dougal and Angus exchanged a look before Dougal relaxed, his big frame slumping back into the too-small café chair. "Hell, it's not that, Sterling. It's good to see you." He shrugged. "And we realize what an opportunity this is for McCarrick Cutting Horses."

Sterling stared at the man, not bothering to hide his skepticism.

All three of them laughed then, the tension slipping away.

"I'd ask you what you've been up to, but I'm guessing busting your ass?" Angus asked, tipping his cowboy hat back. "This is no small job. It's damn impressive, Sterling. I mean it."

"Busting my ass just about covers it." Sterling shifted in the chair, the constant ache in his back dull—but enough to make him stretch a bit. He didn't mind hard work, he preferred it. He didn't do well with time to kill. "Hard work. Perseverance. A good eye when it comes to livestock. And, you know, my natural good looks and charm." He touched his crooked nose, grinning.

"You own a mirror?" Angus asked.

That got them laughing again.

"Glad things are working for you." Dougal seemed sincere, so Sterling nodded his thanks.

It was true things were falling into place now, but that was a recent development. For a time, life had seemed to keep knocking Sterling off his feet—then stomping him into the dirt. He'd kept getting right back up, brushing himself off and moving forward. He wasn't a quitter, he never would be—no matter what other people thought.

"When I got the email, you could have knocked me over with a feather." Angus shook his head, patting the table with his hand. "First, hearing from the National Rodeo Company, and then, seeing it was you."

"Not me." Sterling shrugged. "Yvonne sent it—tagged me on it. Trust me, if I'd written it, it wouldn't have been near as lengthy or as professional sounding."

"Yvonne?" Dougal's brows rose.

"Who's Yvonne?" Angus echoed. "She your someone special?"

"She's someone special, all right." Sterling chuckled. "Yvonne is my... If I said secretary, she'd box my ears. Let's just say she keeps me on track. All of us in the office, that is." She was good at her job and about as no-nonsense as they came. Sterling appreciated that.

"That makes sense." Dougal nodded. "It went on a little long. Not that I'm complaining. It was good news."

"Maybe," Angus cautioned his brother. "Hope-fully."

Sterling respected they weren't already count-ing on anything. Dougal was right, this could be a big opportunity for the brothers. Providing live-stock to the National Rodeo Company would put McCarrick Cutting Horses on the map. His job was to scout the animals and, if he thought it'd be a good partnership, negotiate the contracts for all new stock suppliers. Meaning, if the McCarrick brothers wanted in with the NRC—and they'd be fools not to—he was the man that could make all that happen.

It was because he was so thorough that he'd ad-vanced so quickly. He put the job first. He might know the McCarrick brothers, but that wouldn't affect his decision to sign them on for the NRC. The horses and cattle would decide that.

"You still coming Tuesday? Or are we bumping things up?" Angus finished off his coffee.

"Tuesday's still good for me—depending on the storm, that is." Sterling didn't like the look of the sky. He'd heard reports of a winter storm coming, but he got the feeling it was going to be more than the average, light ice-and-snow flurries. He hoped like hell folks in Granite Falls were ready for it.

"Yeah, news is saying it'll hit about sundown." Dougal shot a quick glance at the grey sky through the large picture window "We best be getting back. Make sure we're all shored up for what's coming." He stood, and offered Sterling his hand. "If you want to come out in an unofficial capacity before then, you're welcome."

Sterling shook the man's hand. "I appreciate that."

Angus touched the brim of his hat and the two brothers left the shop.

Sterling watched the brothers walk down the block and climb into their massive truck before heading back to the counter. Armed with a hot coffee and two sausage rolls he returned to his seat to check his emails on his phone. He had nothing to do for a couple of days. Normally, he'd say that was a bad thing. Time on his hands usually landed him in trouble. That's not who he was now. If he were smart, he'd use this time to apologize to Cassie. He'd planned out what he'd say—each and every word. But that was before he'd seen her again... Now? Well, maybe he wasn't ready. Not quite yet.

He'd have himself some more coffee, a few more of those sausage rolls, and figure out when this storm was hitting and if he should look for some sort of entertainment for this fine Saturday evening. And then, tomorrow, he'd find Cassie and hope she'd hear him out.

Chapter Two

Cassie took the ball from the chute. "B 15. B 15." She held the ball up for everyone to see but no one looked up from their bingo cards. She glanced at Reggie, who was writing down each call she made, just in case there was any confusion. Reggie gave her a thumbs-up and started spinning the ball cage again, over and over.

"Who's close?" Cassie smiled at the number of hands that rose. They were only four games in and already her throat was dry. She watched as another ball rolled down the chute and reached for it. "O 3. O 3."

"Bingo!" A voice called out from the back of the room. "I've got bingo. Someone come check my card."

Cassie looked up, scanning the sizable crowd. High winds and plummeting temps hadn't kept folk from coming out this evening. But, even with the heater in the community center working overtime, most of the bingo players were still wearing their coats and hats to stay warm.

Buzz, Cassie's brother, finished inspecting the bingo card. "Looks good to me. Miss Penny Hodges is the winner."

There was a smattering of applause and a whole lot of grumbling as everyone cleared off their bingo cards in preparation for another round.

"Before we get started on a new game, help yourself to some cookies. Courtesy of The Coffee Shop on Main Street." Cassie pointed at the refreshment table that Jenna, Buzz's fiancée, had set up while they'd been playing the last round. "Cookies and hot chocolate. Move around and warm up a bit."

That announcement was followed by the squeak of folding chairs sliding across the laminate floor, the murmur of conversation and a rush of footsteps headed for the table.

"Can I just say this is a little scary? How serious these folk are taking their bingo, I mean." Buzz stood in front of the raised dais where Cassie and Reggie were sitting. "Velma over there, the talky checker at the grocery store, she tried to convince me that the G 4 was an O 4 last time." He shook his head. "She even offered me her reading glasses—like it was my *eyes* that were the problem."

"I know. Velma is quite a shark when it comes to bingo." Cassie shoved her hands into her pockets for warmth. "Watch out for Blanca, too. She's been known to hide an extra card or two."

Buzz shot her an incredulous look. "I can't believe I let you talk me into this."

She rolled her eyes. "We both know *Jenna* talked you into this, not me." A fact she was incredibly thankful for.

"Yeah, right." He waved her words aside. "Whatever." But he spied Jenna, and his whole expression changed. Everything about her brother softened. "I guess I should go grab a cookie before they're all gone?"

"There is an extra box in the kitchen," Reggie whispered, "for the volunteers."

"A whole box, huh?" Buzz rubbed his hands together.

"You'd better leave some for us." Cassie wagged a finger at him. "And make it snappy. They'll be ready to go here pretty quick." Buzz kept nodding as he headed for Jenna.

Cassie had expected tonight to have a low turnout, but from the looks of it, all the regulars were here. On a good evening, most of the senior citizens of Granite Falls—and the surrounding small towns—came to bingo. Other than Celeste Zamora and Dean Hodges, that is. Celeste used to bring her father, but after he passed, she'd continued to come and play on her own.

"I brought you this." Dean held out a water bottle. "I figure you must be getting pretty parched about now."

Cassie took the bottle, ignoring his eager smile. "Thank you, Dean. My throat is a little dry."

"You, too, Reggie." Dean offered Reggie a water bottle.

Cassie glanced up right as the community center doors opened and... She swallowed. *What is he doing here?*

"What's wrong?" Dean turned and stopped, the muscle going rigid in his jaw. "When did he get into town?"

"He came by the coffee shop this morning— nearly ate all of the sausage rolls, too. He asked what was happening around town, so I told him." Reggie paused then. "Sterling something."

"Sterling Ford," Dean grumbled, glancing at Cassie. "You want me to make him leave?"

As sweet as Dean's offer was, Cassie had a hard time picturing how that would work. Dean wasn't a small man, but next to Sterling, he...was. Plus, Sterling never backed down from a fight, even when he should—at least the Sterling she'd known. As far as she knew, Dean had never been in a fight. "No, Dean, that's fine." She smiled. "He has every right to be here. It makes no difference to me."

Dean nodded and returned to his table, his gaze bouncing to Sterling over and over—openly hostile.

After giving herself a good talking-to in the veterinary clinic bathroom, she'd managed to steady herself. He was nothing special—not anymore. Seeing him was a surprise, sure, but it wasn't a big deal. It didn't need to be, anyway. And that's the way she was going to act. Now, everyone else needed to stop making his presence into a thing.

"What the hell?" Buzz's near growl caught Cassie's attention, but it was the way he stomped toward the door that set Cassie in motion.

She jumped down from the dais and hurried across the room to step in front of her brother. "Buzz, darling brother-o-mine, why don't you go eat another cookie and *not* make a scene?" She smiled brightly but pressed her hand against his chest. "Everyone is looking," she added with a whisper.

"Why is he here?" Buzz glowered down at her.

"Why are you asking *me*?" She kept her smile in place. "Presumably to play bingo?"

Buzz snorted.

"That's lovely." Cassie sighed. "Now, how about you go assure your fiancée that all is well, eat a cookie, and we can get back to bingo?"

Buzz snorted again but turned, stalking back

to the refreshment table where a very bewildered-looking Jenna was still serving punch and cookies.

Old Mrs. Baker, who normally checked everyone in, collected entrance fees and handed out bingo cards, was still shuffling toward the refreshment table. It would take a while—possibly even a whole game—before the woman would return to get Sterling taken care of and ready to play. *Assuming he was here to play?* Cassie took a deep breath, kept her smile in place and headed toward the front table. Buzz couldn't do it, Jenna had her hands full and asking Reggie to do it felt like asking too much at this point.

At least he seemed surprised to see her. That was something. Much better than his blank-faced expression from this morning's meeting.

"Hello. You're here for bingo?" She managed to keep smiling. *I'm cool as a cucumber.*

He tapped his fingers on the stack of cards, the corner of his mouth quirking up. "Bingo? I thought this was a hula class."

Cassie blinked, beyond confused. Was he—

"Kidding." He grinned, his brown eyes dancing. "Bingo, it is."

Cassie blinked again, her chest heavy and tight. "How many cards?" Her smile might have slipped a little. Because, really, she wanted to get this over with as quickly as possible.

He eyed the stack of cards. "How many can I play?"

"Three?" She had no idea. "Four?" Mrs. Baker was stacking her plate with cookies, her every movement in slow motion.

"Two." Sterling handed over the cash, took his card and dauber pen.

That was that. She took a deep breath.

"Anywhere?" he asked.

"Anywhere what?" She'd managed to not make direct eye contact until that moment. But now that it had happened, she didn't know how to undo it. It wasn't that she was overcome with a swell of memories, she'd become quite skilled at blocking all that out. It was because Sterling Ford was devilishly handsome. Possibly more handsome than ever before. This morning she'd become alarmingly aware of how much bigger he seemed to be. Muscles and all that. Now she was forced to look at the man who used to flood her with happiness. Being face-to-face with him had her exploring the familiar razor-sharp jaw, heavy-lidded eyes and the not-so-familiar crooked nose—yep, even his crooked nose was sexy.

Whoa, whoa. Sexy was no longer part of her vocabulary when it came to Sterling. Period. Things like calm, cool and collected were all fine. Frustration, irritation, even anger made sense. But her smile was gone and she was feeling anything but cool as a cucumber.

And now he was standing there, his brown eyes sweeping over her leisurely—as if they were alone.

Which we're not. They were in a room full of people milling about them and, likely, listening to everything that was being said. *Not that much was being said.*

"Sterling?" she murmured, annoyed with herself for getting so frazzled. The sight of Mrs. Baker shuffling back, holding a plate piled high with cookies, only added to her anxiety. "Go sit down."

He nodded but made no move to do as she said. "Anywhere?"

"Yes," she practically hissed. "Anywhere." *As long as it is far, far away from me.* It wasn't her imagination, people were *noticing.* Beyond Mrs. Baker, Jenna had hooked arms with Buzz and was saying something to him. Whatever it was, he was nodding—but he didn't necessarily seem happy.

"All right." Sterling carried his bingo supplies up to the front of the room. Right in front of the dais. Right in front of her and directly in her line of sight.

Really?

The cookie frenzy had died down and most everyone had returned to their seats, and there was no help for it. She'd promised Bobbie Doherty she'd cover for him and that's just what she was going to do. It was bingo, easy-peasy. She'd managed to ignore just about every memory she had of Sterling Ford. How much harder could it be to ignore the man himself?

The woman that ran the coffee shop had told him he'd had two options to occupy himself with that evening: bingo at the community center or karaoke down at the Watering Hole. Slim pickings. Since the only singing he did was in the shower, he'd wandered down Main Street, turned on Huckleberry and walked down the sidewalk to the well-kept community center. The parking lot was packed, a sign that he wasn't the only one in Granite Falls who preferred bingo to karaoke— even with the threat of a winter storm coming. He'd no idea Cassie would be here.

Walking in the door, he'd been struck with a sense of homecoming. He'd moved in with his cousin his freshman year of high school. For him, Granite Falls had been a fresh start. When he went to bed, he wasn't worried about waking up to yelling or fighting or the feel of his father's belt cutting into him at the slightest—or no—provocation. No one here had known a thing about him, his father or their mess of a life. Here, none of that existed. He'd joined the rodeo club, made friends and never looked back.

Cassie Lafferty had played a big part in that.

Until he'd screwed everything up.

And, from the look on Buzz Lafferty's face, his screwup hadn't been forgiven or forgotten. Would Buzz have a warmer welcome for him this time? Sterling ran his finger along the break in his nose. Maybe, maybe not.

Sterling was tired. Bone-tired. He didn't want to deal with Buzz or Dean or anyone else looking for a fight. The wiser course of action might be returning the bingo cards and dauber and heading to the Watering Hole. But he wasn't about to break his two-plus year streak. He'd worked too hard to get here. Nothing and no one would change his mind. Even if things were getting damn uncomfortable two games in.

He'd been looking forward to an evening to relax before he tracked down Cassie tomorrow. Instead, he was seated right up front—staring up at Cassie as she called out the bingo numbers. Cassie'd had this thing about her—an energy. She'd been a talker, using her hands and making faces and laughing at her own jokes. Sterling had always liked watching her. Hell, he'd enjoyed being with her. It didn't matter where she was or who she was with, she made things better. But tonight felt different. If anything, she seemed uncomfortable in her own skin. Which was nothing like the Cassie he knew.

He'd been gone so long, he wasn't even a blip on her radar anymore—but he seemed as in tune to her as ever. Something was bothering her.

Over and over, his attention wandered from his bingo card to the woman calling out numbers. She hadn't changed a bit. Not on the outside, anyway. On the inside? He had no way of knowing and no right to find out. The more he looked at her, the more the "what if's" and bone-deep longing fought to resurface.

He'd come to Granite Falls with two goals: decide on the McCarrick Cutting Horses deal and make peace with Cassie. He was not going to let himself start feeling things, things best left forgotten.

Since Buzz Lafferty kept shooting death glares his way and he was more interested in Cassie than either of his bingo cards, he figured clearing out was the best option. Not that he was going to tuck tail and run, no way. He waited, went through the motions and managed not to jump out of his chair and run for the door when someone finally called "bingo." Instead, he wiped off his cards, gathered up his things and carried them back to the table.

"Sterling Ford." Mrs. Baker sat there, munching on Christmas cookies—a sprinkling of red-and-green sugar crystals and cookie crumbs covering a good portion of the table. "I thought it was you. My, son, you've grown into quite a man now, haven't you?" She grinned, her light-up Christmas necklace twinkling red and green and white.

"I eat my vegetables." He winked, patting his stomach.

She cackled. "Well, it's working for you. Last I heard, you were riding bulls all over. What brings you back after all this time?"

Was it possible that no one but Buzz and the McCarrick brothers knew about his short visit three years ago? "Work."

"Oh-ho?" Her brows rose, creasing her forehead like an accordion. "Nothing else?" She peered over the rim of her oversize glasses at him, then Cassie.

"No, ma'am." He grinned. "Nothing else."

Sterling felt a hand clamp down on his shoulder. "Glad to hear it." For the most part, Buzz Lafferty sounded cordial enough.

Sterling turned, shaking the man's hand off. "Buzz."

"Sterling." Buzz's eyes narrowed, but his tight smile remained. "Mighty surprised to see you here tonight."

Sterling glanced over at Cassie. "Oh? I heard bingo was the place to be, so here I am." *Not that I expected to find Cassie here or have her giving me the stink eye all evening.*

Buzz glanced at the stage, then at Mrs. Baker and the cards Sterling had just turned in. "No luck?"

"Nope." Sterling wasn't sure what, exactly, Buzz was referring to. Bingo or Cassie? Either way, the answer was the same.

He hadn't expected Cassie to welcome him back with open arms—he wasn't that big a fool. He'd had his share of head injuries, but he still had his wits about him. Thinking Cassie would ever give him another chance? No. No way. It hurt like hell, but the fault was all his and he had to live with that. Apologizing to her was all he dared hope for. But even that might be asking too much.

"Evening, Mrs. Baker. Buzz." He touched the brim of his hat. "I'll let you get back to it." He headed for the doors, hoping like hell Buzz would leave it be. As soon as he stepped outside, he zipped up his coat and shoved his hands into his pockets. His breath turned to vapor in the cold. *The temperature's dropping all right.*

Sterling was halfway down the block when Buzz caught up to him.

"Hold up." Buzz's tone was warning enough. Buzz Lafferty was spoiling for a fight.

If Sterling explained why he was here, that would be the end of it. Buzz would have no cause to be upset, and the whole damn thing would be over and done with. But Sterling had every right to be here and just as much a right to be pissed at Buzz. If Buzz wanted a fight, he was in for a shock. This time, Sterling would fight back. For now, he waited with his hands in his pockets.

Buzz shook his head. "Listen… I know things were bad last time you were here—"

"It was quite a welcome," Sterling agreed.

"I… I'm sorry for that." Buzz mumbled. "It was bad timing. Cassie had been through hell and back and… But he was gone and you show up… That beating was meant for him. Not that you were innocent, mind you." He shook his head. "And not that any of that is your business," he murmured the last. "Dammit."

Sterling's chest grew tight. He didn't like what Buzz was implying. What had Cassie been through? Who was *he*? And why the hell had Buzz let the bastard that hurt her go? Technically, Buzz was right and it was none of his business. But that didn't stop the questions from rolling in or the surge of anger that gripped him by the throat. "What about Angus? Dougal?" Standing there, watching. Dougal only stepped in when Sterling was exhausted, his nose was broken and he was seeing stars. Then the two brothers had followed him all the way out of town—to make sure he left.

"It was wrong. I won't make any excuses." Buzz frowned. "You know they're just as protective of Cassie as I am. They were there when, well, it doesn't matter. They were just as wound up as I was." He shook out his arms, his hands clenching—and his voice going low and gruff. "I can't explain it. I've never felt that way, and damn it all, I hope I never feel that way again." He took a deep breath. "I'm not excusing it." His gaze was long and hard. "I was wrong."

Sterling swallowed hard. Whatever anger or resentment he'd felt turned to ash in his mouth, leaving a bitter taste on his tongue and his stomach churning. What had happened? And who was the bastard responsible? Why the hell hadn't Buzz, Angus, and Dougal stopped whatever was happening? They should have known. If they'd been doing their damn job protecting her, then. how had this happened? A new anger heated his blood. Not for what Buzz had done to him but for what Buzz hadn't prevented from happening to Cassie.

"But…" Buzz cleared his throat. "I'm Cassie's brother. It's my job to protect her."

Sterling managed not to point out Buzz needed to do a better job, but it was hard.

"I told myself if you ever came through town again, I'd apologize." Buzz took a deep breath. "For throwing punches—not for what I said."

Sterling couldn't stop the chuckle from slipping out. "I guess I shouldn't admit I don't recall much of what was said."

Hands on hips, Buzz straightened. "Oh? I guess I'll give you a quick refresher. Cassie is off-limits. You two don't fit—you want different things—"

"All I ever wanted was her." Sterling didn't know why he said it.

Buzz stepped forward, his voice low. "If that was true, she wouldn't have second-guessed herself nine times out of ten or cried herself to sleep for damn near a year after you left."

With a whoosh, the air was knocked from Sterling's lungs, followed by a one-two kick to the throat. How many of those nights had he been passed-out drunk, who knows where—aching— for her? It gutted him to think he'd hurt her like that. He'd hurt so many people. He'd hurt Cassie worst of all. He'd been so messed up in the head, so angry at the world, he'd acted like a damn fool and lost her. *And left her for some son of a bitch who did who knows what to wound her all over again.*

"I don't think you've come back here for her. It's been six years since you've seen her—you've both moved on." Buzz wasn't asking.

Only because you stopped me from seeing her three years ago.

"Buzz?" Cassie's voice reached them, carried on a gust of icy wind. "Is everything okay?"

"Fine," Buzz called back. "Just fine." He blew into his hands and rubbed them together.

But Sterling wasn't looking at the man in front of him, not anymore. His attention was drawn, as always, to the woman standing outside the community center. Her strawberry blond hair was aglow beneath the fluorescent light over the doors. Her denim skirt was fitted, skimming curves that damn near tore a groan of appreciation from him. She wore a plain white shirt and brown cowboy boots, and all of it—all of her—had him struggling for breath all over again. It was too cold. She shouldn't be out here without a jacket.

"Sterling?" Cassie's voice wavered just enough to send a shiver down his spine.

"Just catching up is all." He touched the brim of his hat. "Been a while."

"Yes." Cassie hugged herself. "It has."

Go inside before you freeze. Sterling pressed his lips tight to keep the words inside.

"I'm coming." Buzz turned and headed back to

his sister. "Knowing that crew, they'll start rioting if you don't get the next game started."

"Reggie broke out more cookies." Cassie laughed.

Buzz held the door to the community center open, but Cassie hesitated, staring into the growing dark—at him. "Cassie?" Buzz urged.

"Right." Cassie murmured something else, but Sterling was too far away to hear her. With a swish of long hair, she was gone and the doors closed.

He stood there, staring at the doors, with pressure building up inside his chest. For a split second, it felt like he'd gone back in time. If he'd been smarter, he never would have let his father get into his head—and he sure as hell wouldn't have left. He'd have listened to her when she asked him to stay. *But I didn't.* Apologizing to Cassie wouldn't erase what he'd done or said that nightmare of a day so long ago, but he hoped it would make the regret he'd shouldered ever since a little easier to carry.

Chapter Three

Cassie stood, her apron tied at the waist, placed two pieces of chocolate on Reggie's freshly made croissant-roll dough and carefully rolled it up. "Like this?" she asked.

"Perfect." Reggie nodded. "Y'all are the best. Seriously. I don't know what I would have done without you all."

"That's the thing about small towns, we help each other out." Cassie shrugged.

"Unless we don't like you," Skylar added, laughing.

"But we like you." Jenna, Buzz's fiancée, was quick to reassure.

"And we love your pastries," Monica, Jenna's teenage sister, added.

"You can take home as much as you want." Reggie gave Monica a wink.

"Maybe not as much as you want." Jenna shook her head, shooting Reggie a warning look. "Remember how many mouths I have to feed—then add that much again for Buzz."

"True." Cassie nodded. "My brother has a hollow leg. It's the only way he can eat that much and stay trim."

"Kyle is the same." Skylar sighed. "It's just not fair."

There was a general ripple of agreement in the kitchen, followed by smiles and laughter. The temps kept dropping and the wind had picked up, but the only damage, so far, was a downed power line on Main Street. Reggie's place and the two shops next door had lost power. Granite Falls wasn't a big town, so the public utility vehicles were doing the best they could. Several neighborhoods across town were without power—they took precedence over Main Street. When Cassie had received Reggie's panicked call about her refrigerator going out and all the dough that was going to go bad, Cassie had started making calls of her own. Now the community center's industrial kitchen was full of helping hands and the most delicious smells.

"I'm glad this won't all go to waste." Reggie spread a thick cinnamon-sugar paste onto a large rectangle of thick dough. "Good thing you're so connected, Cassie."

"Good thing I still had the key to the community center, you mean." Cassie laughed, rolled up another croissant, carefully moved it to the parchment-lined cookie sheet, then pinched the ends into the expected croissant shape. Once they'd rallied and taken inventory on the sheer amount of food that was in danger, Cassie had come up with a plan. Now they were making goodie baskets for the teacher's lounge at all three campuses as well as several more to deliver to the Granite Falls Senior Living and Retirement Community. Not only would their efforts make sure there was no food wasted, it would be a great way for Reggie to reach new customers.

"I can't thank you enough." Reggie stopped running the pizza cutter along the dough in nice, even cuts. "All of you."

Once they'd hauled everything from the restaurant to the community center, it was easy. After several hours of work, the long, metal, kitchen countertops were covered with white butcher's paper and cooling racks stacked high with blueberry and orange scones, sausage rolls, cookies of all varieties and berry tarts. Jenna and Monica had set about putting together baker's boxes and white paper sleeves for packaging. All that was left were the croissants, chocolate croissants and cinnamon rolls.

"There's no way I would've been able to get half as much done, cooking at home." Reggie rolled up the strips of dough into fist-sized cinnamon rolls.

"You make that look so easy." Monica frowned, eyeing her own rolls in disappointment.

"It just takes practice." Reggie smiled. "No one cares how they look as long as they taste good. And remember, gooey frosting covers all imperfections." She winked at Monica. "Now that we're mostly done, I have an important question to ask."

"What question?" Cassie used a pastry brush to egg wash the croissants.

Skylar helped move cinnamon rolls onto another industrial-sized cookie sheet.

"Fire away." Jenna nodded, heading to the sink to wash her hands.

"Last night, at bingo… I got the impression that there's a…a *story* about Sterling Ford?" Reggie grinned. "When he came in here yesterday, he sat at the counter and chatted and all I could think was, wow, he is so good-looking. And then there was some *tension*."

Hopefully, Reggie was one of the only people that picked up on it.

Skylar glanced Cassie's way. "I think I've heard his name mentioned, but I can't quite place where."

"He used to be a bull rider." Cassie kept her eyes on her croissants, taking extreme care with her egg wash. "He had a promising start—highly ranked and winning big purses." Until his monster of a father pushed him too hard...*no matter how I tried to warn him.* Cassie swallowed hard. She didn't know why he'd dropped off the rankings board and then off the rodeo circuit altogether. After he'd left Granite Falls, it had taken her a long time to feel remotely human. Trying to keep up with him or track his career would get in the way of that. To protect herself, she avoided any and all news about Sterling. "He lived here, back in high school. We dated, actually."

"You did?" Reggie nudged her. "Lucky you."

Cassie smiled. She'd thought so—when she'd been naive and blinded by love.

"Buzz had a few things to say about him." Jenna leaned against the counter, wiping her hands on her apron.

"Boy, did he." Monica sighed. "He really doesn't like him. Like, really, really."

"Oh?" Skylar glanced at Cassie. "Buzz is normally so...chill. I'm guessing this Sterling guy is a jerk?"

"According to Buzz, he's like king of the jerks." Monica nodded. "He said they even got into a fight once."

Cassie frowned. "They did?" This was the first she was hearing about it. As far as she knew, Buzz had been just as hurt when Sterling left and ceased all communications.

"That's what he said." Jenna was frowning. "Maybe it was a secret."

"Oops." Monica covered her mouth.

"It's okay." Was it? Cassie tried to piece things together. Buzz and Sterling fighting? When? Until now, she and her brother didn't have any secrets. *This felt like a pretty big secret.* But all eyes were on her, so she forced a smile. "All that was so long ago. I'm sure it just slipped his mind." Unlikely, but she was prepared to let it go. It didn't matter now. "I haven't seen Sterling in, oh, at least six years."

"I get the feeling we're not talking some teen-age crush?" Skylar asked, watching Cassie.

"Yeah...me, too." Reggie, too, was looking at her. "I didn't mean to bring up bad memories, Cassie."

They weren't all bad memories. Cassie treasured some. He'd been her everything. She'd believed in their love and their future together. Until he was gone. Until he'd said all those horrible things about her holding him back—and not believing in him.

"I'm sensing the need to change the subject." Jenna's hand rested on Cassie's shoulder. "But, you know, if you ever want to talk about it—not just about your hot ex-boyfriend—you've got people willing to listen." She winked.

"Definitely," Skylar agreed.

"Samesies." Reggie nudged her. "I know I'm new here, barely six months, but I've got your back, Cassie. I studied krav maga and tae kwon do before I moved to Granite Falls. If this Sterling Ford deserves to be put in his place again, it doesn't matter how hot he is, I'll be first in line."

"Ooh, can you teach me some moves?" Monica leaned forward with interest.

Cassie laughed as Reggie and Monica turned the tide of conversation from Sterling to self-defense. It was a much safer subject, but she couldn't quite shake the feeling that Buzz had been hiding things from her. If she asked him, would he tell her or remain silent while saying he was doing what was best for her?

"If a date ever gets too handsy, you'll be able to put him in his place." Reggie grinned.

"Yeah, well, I love Buzz and all, and I'm glad he's marrying my sister, but he's superprotective and it makes me wonder if I'll ever be able to date, like, ever." Monica rolled her eyes and heaved a big sigh.

Reggie and Skylar laughed.

"You're thirteen." Jenna's smile had just a

touch of concern. "A little young to date, don't you think?"

Cassie had been Monica's age when she'd first laid eyes on Sterling. She remembered it like it was yesterday. He'd been all smiles and bad jokes and she'd fallen head over heels. *And look where it landed me.* Still, it wasn't fair to assume Monica would end up in the same situation.

"I didn't say I wanted to, not yet." Monica shrugged, her cheeks a deep pink. "I just said *when* I do, you're going to have to back me up, Jenna. You're my sister, after all."

"When you do, I'm pretty sure Alonzo will be waiting to ask you out." Reggie smiled at Monica, who turned a deeper red.

"He's a sweet boy." Jenna sighed. "And he's been a good *friend* to you. But he needs to wait a little longer for anything else."

"It's good advice." Cassie set her brush aside. "Boys can wait. If he's really interested, he won't mind waiting on you either."

"Yeah, I guess." But Monica's disappointment was obvious.

While Jenna and Skylar helped Reggie bring out the baskets, colored plastic wrap and over-size twist ties, Cassie drew the girl into a hug and whispered, "If you really, really want to date this boy—*when* it's time—I'll help you with my brother."

"You're awesome, Cassie." Monica threw her arms around her neck. "I'm so lucky to have you for my aunt. Almost-aunt." She laughed as she let Cassie go, then shrugged. "Well, you know what I mean." She smiled up at her. "And if this Sterling guy doesn't know how awesome you are, then I'm glad Buzz beat him up and chased him out of town."

Cassie gave her another quick hug before helping with the gift basket assembly line, but her brain was replaying what Monica had said. *Chased him off...* Buzz had chased Sterling off? *And* fought with him? Had this really happened? Buzz would have no reason to lie about it. She swallowed. *And why does any of it still matter?*

Sterling backed out of the Frosty King, his cell phone wedged between his shoulder and his ear, alternating answering Yvonne's questions and enjoying his triple-scoop, chocolate-chip ice cream cone. It was cold, and most folk were getting hot chocolate, but Sterling was a man of habit. A Frosty King triple-scoop, chocolate-chip ice cream cone hit the spot every time. A large family was coming in so he held the door wide.

"They want to negotiate the final payouts."

And, from the sound of it, Yvonne wasn't happy about it. "This is the third time they've come back with changes, Sterling."

"Email the contract to me and don't let them get to you, Yvonne. If they're going to keep giving you the runaround, I'm not so sure we need to be pursuing any sort of contract with them." He lifted his cone to catch the chocolate dripping off his hand.

"I like it when you talk tough." Yvonne laughed.

"Thank you," the mother of the large family whispered, steering her stroller inside.

Sterling nodded in acknowledgement before telling Yvonne, "I only get tough when I have to." He chuckled. "If you say I have to, I believe it." He let the door go and turned, dodging a life-size, Nutcracker, tinsel-and-lights soldier and slamming into something. Or someone. His ice cream splatted, his phone slipped free, and he was staring down into the round and very startled eyes of Cassie Lafferty. Cassie, who had ice cream on her cheek, her chin and smack-dab in the middle of her chest.

"Cassie." Sterling reached into his back pocket for his bandana. "I am so sorry." He wiped at her cheek, managing to smear it.

"It's fine." She blinked, staring down at her chest. "Oh." She shivered, swiping at the coldness with her glove-covered fingers. "Ick." She eyed the ice cream mess on her gloves.

"It's not fine." He shook his head. "Dammit."

"Why are you eating ice cream?" Cassie glanced up at him. "It's thirty degrees out."

"It sounded good. I should've been looking at where I was going, hung up the damn phone and paid attention." He wiped her chin, sighing.

"I'm not going to argue." She shivered in the cold air, but her gaze was fixed on his face.

"I didn't mean to..." His words fizzled out as she continued to stare at him. He had no idea what she was thinking. Was she mad? Could be. Sad? Possibly. Irritated? That was another distinct possibility. "Sorry," he murmured.

"Accidents happen." She inhaled, her breath unsteady, as her eyes shifted to the sticky patch on her coat. "I can take it from here."

He handed over the bandana. "I've got another one." He held up his finger and stepped off the curb, hurrying to his truck. He opened the door, leaned in, and pulled his duffel bag into the front seat. He had another bandana. Somewhere. He pulled out some jeans, tossed aside some clean socks and rifled around inside.

"Sterling. It's fine." Cassie stood on the sidewalk, attempting to dislodge the goo that was clinging to her coat.

He grabbed for one of his shirts. "Here." He held it out.

Cassie shook her head.

"It's the least I can do." He stepped closer.

"Your phone." She held it out. "Some woman is yelling your name."

"Yvonne." He sighed. He'd worry about that later.

"It's cracked." She nodded at the screen. "But I could hear Yvonne, so maybe it still works."

He didn't give a damn about the phone. The company paid for it, they'd get him a new one. "Trade me."

She sighed but took the shirt. "Thank you."

Before he could say another word, she turned and disappeared inside the Frosty King. He stared after her, feeling every bit the ass. He hadn't exchanged ten sentences with the woman, but he'd doused her with his triple scoop of ice cream easy enough. He'd add that to the list of things he had to apologize for.

He slammed his hat on the driver's seat, ran his fingers through his hair and considered his options. Go in after her, wait for her here, or leave and try again later. Just about the time he'd decided to go in after her, she came out—her coat damp and his shirt dangling from her fingers.

He hadn't realized which shirt he'd handed her

until now. But now that she was holding it out, his mind decided to make it ten times worse and drag up every memory he had related to that shirt. Cassie at the river, wearing that shirt when her shoulders got too pink. Cassie with Bert and Ernie as tiny puppies, wrapped up in that shirt. Cassie sleeping over, wearing his shirt and nothing else.

"I can't believe you still own this." She held it with her fingertips only, at arms' length. "It's pretty bare in a few places."

"It's got plenty of wear left in it." At least that's what he kept telling himself. He knew why he held on to it and why every time he tried to get rid of the damn thing, he'd go dig it out of the trash.

Cassie's gaze bounced to his face, then back to the garment in question.

"You think...? Can I buy you an ice cream?" Sterling slammed his truck door.

Cassie frowned. "I don't know. Can you be trusted with another cone?" Her frown melted, leaving a smile that made the hollow spot in his chest ache something fierce.

He cleared his throat. "You'll be happy to know I have at least four more clean shirts—just in case."

Her smile wavered. Because she didn't want to be here with him. Since his arrival in Granite

Falls yesterday, she'd made it clear she'd no interest in spending time with him.

"If you're free." He shook his head. "If you've got plans—"

"No." She swallowed, barely looking at him.

"No." He paused. "No to the ice cream or no—"

"I don't have plans." She finished. "Not for a while." She walked to the door of the Frosty King, waiting for him.

It took a minute for him to realize she'd said yes. She'd said yes and she was waiting for him to follow her. He tossed the shirt into his truck and hurried to open the door for her. Other than the large group of children and their very tired-looking mother, the place was empty.

"Hey?" The same teenager that had served him earlier was standing behind the counter.

"I dropped it." He gave her a rueful grin.

"I was gonna say. I like ice cream, but even I wouldn't be back so soon. Plus, you're the only person ordering ice cream today." She smiled. "What can I get you this time?"

"Double scoop of chocolate and…" He glanced at Cassie. "You still like Neapolitan best?"

Cassie went stiff, took a deep breath, then nodded. "But I'd rather have hot chocolate." She paused. "And extra napkins, please. Lots of them."

"Very funny." But Sterling was laughing.

They took their order and sat at the table in the corner—in absolute silence. Every time he started to say something, he locked up.

"Sterling?" Cassie had been studying each of the framed ice cream prints that decorated the walls of the tiny shop, but she was staring at him now. "Can I ask a question?"

He nodded.

"I heard something earlier this morning and I was hoping you could clear things up for me?" She blew on her hot chocolate, then took a small sip.

"I guess." He couldn't help but brace himself a bit.

"I was helping Reggie put together some care packages this morning, with friends, and someone mentioned that you and Buzz had a fight?"

He nodded. "Sort of."

"How do you 'sort of' fight?" Cassie's brow furrowed.

"A fight, in my mind, is between two opponents." He shrugged, licking his ice cream. "I never raised a hand against Buzz."

"You didn't fight back?" Her cup stopped halfway to her mouth.

"He's your brother." He shrugged. "I figured, after everything, I'd deserved it."

"So, it *did* happen?" The furrow grew deeper. "And did he…did he chase you out of town?"

Sterling shook his head, his gaze dropping to his ice cream. "There was no point in staying. Buzz made it clear you'd moved on and I wasn't welcome. Angus, too."

She held up her hand. "Wait. I'm confused." She opened her mouth, closed it, then asked, "When did this happen?"

Right about then, Sterling felt the hair on the back of his neck prick up. "When I was here last."

"And when...when would that have been?" Cassie's hand, and her ice cream, were shaking. "Six years ago? When we broke up? Right?"

"No. I came back about three years ago." He leaned forward.

"You were here three years ago?" She was staring at him in open confusion.

"You didn't know?" He'd hoped as much. All this time he'd wondered which would be worse— Buzz jumping in to stop him with her blessing or her never knowing he'd come to see her.

"No." She was shaking her head. "No, I didn't know. Why were you here?"

"I..." He cleared his throat. "I came to see you."

Cassie seemed to be looking for something, but she kept her thoughts to herself. Her gaze dipped from his. When her eyes met his, the telltale sheen of tears grabbed him by the throat and held on. She stood, tossing her hot chocolate cup into the trash, and wiped her hands on napkin after napkin. "I should go." But she stayed, staring at him like she had so much more to say.

If he'd thought it through, he wouldn't have stood or caught her hand or murmured her name. But he did, all of it. Staring down at her. Brushing his thumb over her silky hand. Her name damn near spilling from his lips. It was a fool move on his part—one that had instant and dire consequences.

Cassie's breath caught and she yanked away, like his touch burned her, and she all but ran from the ice cream parlor. Sterling watched her go, cursing himself. *What the hell was I thinking?* He sank into his chair, blood roaring in his ears and his hands fisting on his thighs.

He'd come to Granite Falls with a plan. Work came first—it was the only constant he had. First up, determining whether or not to sign the McCarricks as livestock contractors. It was pretty straightforward. Then he'd talk to Cassie—to apologize. Nowhere, in any of that, had he considered that seeing her might stir up long-forgotten feelings and dreams.

He took a deep breath and stared at the holiday decorations painted on the windows of the Frosty King. Nothing had changed. He would always be the asshole that'd let drink and insecurity push her away. He hated that he'd shut her out, not the questions and fears his father had spent years drilling into his brain.

He'd tried to block out the day he'd ended it—it helped that he'd already started drinking that morning. What he did remember was bad enough. He'd slammed doors and punched a wall. He'd said she'd only been with him because she felt sorry for him *and* she thought she could change him into something better. Worse, she didn't believe in him, so there was no way she'd ever truly loved him. The thing is, he'd believed what he was saying. He'd believed his father had his best interests at heart. It'd taken months before Sterling realized his father was full of shit. By then, he'd been drinking too much to care.

That was another lifetime. He'd come here knowing he'd hurt her too much to expect anything from her. He'd be damn lucky if she forgave him for all that he'd done and said to her. But he couldn't ignore the sinking feeling that, if he wasn't careful, his battered heart would be in pieces all over again by the time he left Granite Falls.

Chapter Four

Cassie had her heat on full blast, Christmas music blaring from her small SUV's speakers and her foot hovering over the brakes. She was a ball of nerves. Leaning over her steering wheel to peer out the front windshield was no help. And even with her headlights on high beams, visibility was tricky.

"You two okay?" She peered into the rearview mirror to find Bert and Ernie sitting up, ears perked and tongues lolling—with no care in the world. She eyed the cardboard box filling the passenger seat beside her. "I would ask you two, but you look like you're sleeping so..." The box of tiny puppies had been dropped off by a trucker passing through town. He'd found them alone in the bathroom stall in a highway rest stop but didn't have the time to take care of two close-eyed, wriggling little pups. Cassie, on the other hand, had time to hand feed them, keep them warm and play Momma dog for as long as needed. She was so glad he'd brought them to her.

Bert made a low rumble in his throat, so Cassie glanced in the rearview mirror—to see Bert nosing around one of the gift baskets. "Keep your noses to yourselves, boys."

Ernie shot her a look, as if he was offended she'd lumped him into her reprimand.

Cassie had offered to deliver several of the gift packages they'd spent the morning assembling, but now that the norther had hit, she wasn't sure when the deliveries would happen. *I'll be happy if we make it home.*

Sleet and rain tap-tapped on the hood of her small SUV. Wind gusts pushed her vehicle around and the road was already getting slick—and she was nowhere close to home.

"Maybe we should have stayed at the vet hospital." She glanced back at Bert and Ernie. Now, with the wind and snow and ice picking up, she was seriously regretting her decision. Buzz and Jenna's place was another option, but she'd have to put up with Buzz and his concerned, Sterling-focused questions and long, assessing looks until the weather cleared. Cassie wasn't up for that.

"We can do it." She flexed her fingers and tried to relax. "Slow and steady."

But her confidence took a nosedive when she hit a patch of black ice and her SUV spun out, crossed into the opposite lane and slid onto the shoulder of the road, throwing out an arm to keep the box of puppies safe as the vehicle tipped forward and down the embankment to slam to a stop. The front end of her small SUV folded up on itself once it careened into an immovable cedar-post fence.

Cassie saw stars. The force of impact slammed her against the steering wheel and pulled her seat belt tight against her chest and shoulder. She sucked in air, grateful breathing didn't hurt. Her head was a different story. She'd smacked into the driver's window—cracking the pane and leaving her with a constant pulse in her temples.

Wind roared outside. Pricks of ice stung her cheek and neck. And the temperature inside her car began to plummet. She peeled her fingers off the box of puppies beside her. Both of them were wriggling and squeaking, but the towels and blankets she'd used to keep them warm had also kept them bundled up and safe.

"Boys?" Her words were more grunt than anything. "You okay?" She unbuckled and turned.

Bert and Ernie instantly leaned forward, the two of them sniffing her head and face and whimpering.

"I'm okay." She reached up, giving them each a reassuring ear rub. "We'll be okay." She used her baby voice, hoping to soothe them. "We just need

to figure things out. Like how to get out of here."
The longer she sat here, the more aware she was
of her current state. She wasn't as okay as she'd
like to be. There was a viselike grip at the base of
her skull, shooting pain into her head and putting
pressure behind her eyes.

She pressed a hand against her left shoulder and
winced. She'd never been so thankful for the puffy
ski coat she'd bought on clearance years ago. Not
that she'd ever been skiing. The coat had likely
provided some buffer. Yes, her shoulder hurt. Her
chest hurt. But it could have been so much worse.
She blinked, her head truly throbbing now.

Her gaze swept over the contents of the cab. Her
purse was on the passenger floorboard, the contents spilled out and all over—but she, the dogs
and the puppies were safe. "Thank goodness we're
all okay."

She smiled as Ernie whimpered, nudging her
ear with his nose. "Don't worry." She took a deep
breath and tried to stay calm. "A plan. We need a
plan." The temperature was below freezing. She
needed to find her phone and call for help. She
shifted slowly, bracing her feet against the floorboard as she leaned over to search for her phone.

"It's here." She murmured. "I know it's here."
Her hands were shaking, her fingers aching from
the cold. All she found was a half a dozen brightly
colored lipsticks, her journal, her wallet, a handful

of caramel hard candies and some hand sanitizer. "Where is it?" She pushed forward, slamming her boot-covered feet harder against the driver's side floorboard as she reached over the passenger edge to feel along the door panel.

That's when she heard it. The crunch.

She sat up, the sudden movement leaving her so dizzy she gripped the steering wheel. Nausea washed over her, her hands clammy and her throat tight. This wasn't good. A few shallow breaths. A few more seconds to find balance. And she peered down at the driver's floorboard, between her feet.

"There's my phone." She groaned. "Or what's left of it." The glass screen was cracked and dark. It wasn't a huge surprise when the phone didn't turn on or let her dial for help, but it did nothing to ease her mounting panic. There wasn't time to cry or feel sorry for herself. And really, her head hurt too much as it was. Crying would only make it worse. "Okay. Plan B." She injected as much cheerfulness into her voice as she could.

She hadn't cleaned out the rear of her car in some time. Buzz was always giving her grief about it. At the moment, she was grateful. She had a few emergency items in her hatch—there would be things she could use. Surely. She used one of the extra towels she'd brought along to cover the puppy box. "Hopefully it'll keep them warm for a bit." She gave Bert, then Ernie a quick pat. "You boys stay put. Stand guard." She opened her door and shielded her face. The wind was so strong it flung the door wide. "Stay." She held her hand out. "Stay," she said again, smiling when they both sat on the back seat. She flipped on the car's blinking hazard lights and slid out, shaking the few glass pebbles from the cracked windshield off her coat and stomping to free any pieces clinging to her jeans. "Thank goodness for laminated glass." The stomping and shaking didn't help the lingering dizziness, but time was of the essence—she had to focus and *do* something. Now. She pushed the front door shut and steadied herself.

The ground crunched beneath her boots. The ice-capped grass was slick enough that she had to brace a hand along the side of her vehicle, planting each step firmly so she wouldn't fall. By the time she opened the hatch, she was shivering and dizzy and panic was beginning to creep in.

It'll be okay. She rifled through her emergency box, finding a reflective road triangle alongside her tire iron and jack. If anyone dared to be out and about on the roads on a night like tonight, that would come in handy. She grabbed it, her waterproof picnic blanket, a flashlight, a roll of duct tape, a sleeping bag and yoga mat, then slammed the hatch door. A little too hard in this cold. The hatch window shattered and sent shards straight at her. She felt a few stings on her temple and the inside of her hand and wrists as she tried to protect herself. It was so cold, she could barely feel the new cuts. And, anyway, she didn't have time to worry over them—not when the storm was getting worse.

"Here." She dropped the waterproof picnic blanket and sleeping bag into the back seat. "Stay warm. I'll cuddle you two in just a minute."

Even with numb fingers and shaky hands, she managed to tape her yoga mat over the hatchback window. "There." It wasn't going to warm things up, but at least it would keep the wind out. She pushed against the tape and made sure she was satisfied before moving on.

"Next." She moved slowly, carefully away from the car to the embankment. Leaning forward to brace her hands along the slope helped her climb to the road. Thankfully, it wasn't steep—her head was splitting and the world seemed to be getting more and more crooked as she went. She set the reflective triangle up and placed it on the road's shoulder—bracing it with a sizeable rock so it wouldn't blow away. The bright orange reflector triangle was close enough to the road that any headlights would bounce off and alert drivers. From where she stood, she could see the flashing of her hazard lights. *Someone will find us.* But she paused, staring one way, then the other. Other than the wind, it was quiet. No car or truck engines. No birds. No crickets. Nothing but the howling wind and the steady, brittle tap of sleet falling from the sky to hit the icy ground.

This was bad.

Really bad.

But there was nothing else she could do, so...

She half slid back down the embankment, took slow hard steps through the ice to the car, then pulled the back passenger door open. Bert and Ernie stood up from their huddle as she collapsed the back seats, greeting her with tail wags and whimpers. "Make room for me and the puppies." She slid in, pulled the door closed and pulled the box of puppies over and next to her. She did her best to cocoon them in the waterproof picnic blanket and sleeping bag. Bert burrowed against one side and Ernie the other, while the box rested in her lap. It wasn't exactly warm, but it was enough to take the edge off the cold.

Please, please, let someone find us.

Her head felt so heavy she could barely lift it. So she didn't. She relaxed against the seat, curled into her dogs and let the exhaustion roll over her.

Sterling kept his speed steady, lifting his foot off the pedal every time his wheels slipped on the ice. Yvonne had rented a cabin through one of those home rental sites. She knew he liked his space and thought this was a better option than the B and B in town. He'd appreciated it at the time, but now, with this storm, he wasn't so sure. To say this was unusual Texas weather was an understatement.

According to his phone's GPS, he only had a few miles to go.

He cruised along, eyes narrowed, his windshield wipers knocking aside the snow and giving him a few precious moments of visibility. It was dark. An inky and starless night. White snow. Not much else. And no light beyond the beam of his headlights.

Swish-swish. Swish-swish. Orange.

He frowned, slowing.

Yep. An orange reflector. An emergency, reflective triangle. He edged along the side of the road, shifting his truck into low gear and slowing a few feet from the triangle. His gaze swept the road, then along the sides and down the slight embankment—a vehicle, its hazard lights flashing.

"Damn." The way the car was sitting, it looked like it'd plowed into the fence. Probably slid across the road. Hopefully, everyone was okay. He pulled on his thick, all-weather coat, tugged on his leather gloves, tucked a flashlight into his pocket and climbed down from the cab of his four-wheel-drive work truck.

He slipped on the embankment, landing hard on his ass, but got right back up.

That's when he heard barking. One. No, two dogs. Maybe more. But no one called out. He moved a little faster then. Had the animals been left? Or was their owner injured?

"Hello?" He called out, knocking on the side of the car. "Is everyone okay?"

The barking grew more frantic. One dog let out a long, low sort of bray.

"I'm going to open the door." He reached for the handle. "I'm here to help." He opened the door slowly—and froze.

Bert and Ernie, in full protective mode, stood on either side of a dozing Cassie. Cassie. Who had blood on her face and hand and neck. It wasn't the cold that sliced through him, it was fear. "Cassie?" he murmured, forcing himself to focus. "It's all right, boys." He held his hands out. "Bert. Ernie. It's me. It's all right. I won't hurt you."

Both dogs started to whimper then, nudging Cassie and looking at him.

"I know. Your momma is hurt." And seeing her still and pale plunged him into a level of panic he'd never encountered. "Cassie?" He spoke gently, almost pleading. She had to be okay. She had to. He wouldn't accept anything less. "Cassie Lafferty, you answer me."

Cassie's forehead creased. "Don't boss me." The words were thin and breathy.

He smiled, relief almost bringing him to his knees. That was all Cassie. "Then, wake up and put me in my place."

She didn't respond this time.

"Cassie." He reached in. "Come on, now."

She pulled away from him, curling around the box in her lap and tugging the sleeping bag in close.

"Cassie." He swallowed, leaning in. "We need to get Bert and Ernie someplace warm."

"Yes." Her eyes fluttered then but didn't stay open. "The puppies…"

He scanned her face. The cuts on her temple weren't bleeding. Or her hand. How long had they been out here like this? It was freezing—it had been for six hours or more. "I'm going to get Bert and Ernie someplace warm."

"Yes," she whispered, nodding once.

Of course she'd care more about the dogs than herself. He, on the other hand, wanted to make sure she was okay to move. His years on the rodeo circuit had exposed him to all sorts of injuries. If she'd hurt her neck or back… Well, he had to know. "Cassie? Can you move your fingers?" He waited until she did "jazz hands," then asked,

"What about your toes?" He rested his hands on her boots, relieved to feel her toes pressing against the softened leather. "Good."

She murmured something unintelligible.

"Let's go." He used the sleeping bag to pull her closer. "I'm going to carry you."

"I can walk." There was just the hint of sass.

"Uh-huh." He lifted her into his arms and held her tight against him.

"Puppies," she whimpered, stiffening. "Watch out."

He stared down at the box she was clutching. "Puppies?" He lifted the corner of the towel long enough to see what did, indeed, look like two very young, wriggling puppies. "Okay. And the puppies." He shifted Cassie to allow for room for the puppies, then eyed the dogs watching his every move. "I'll be back, boys." He didn't know if the dogs were hurt or if either needed carrying, but first things first. Cassie needed shelter and warmth. "Don't worry, I've got her." He pushed the door closed, and their whimpers grew muffled.

"Shh. You're so loud. You'll wake them up." She leaned her head against his chest, clutching the box to her tightly, and turning so her nose was pressed against his coat front. "I like this dream." Her body seemed to ease, going lax against him.

"Dream?" He wished like hell this was a dream.

His heart was damn near beating out of his chest, but he didn't stop moving. He stepped carefully, making his way up the ice-slick hill to his waiting truck. He shifted her against his shoulder and managed to open the passenger door. "I'd like it a whole hell of a lot better if you weren't hurt." He wasn't sure if his words reached her or not. "I'll get the dogs now. But you and the puppies are safe now. And warm. You hear me?" He paused. "Anything else in the car I need to get? Cassie?"

"Uh, baskets." Her eyes popped open, but she was bleary-eyed and distant. "Gift baskets. Dog food. Puppy formula. You know, that stuff..." She blinked rapidly until her eyes closed.

First puppies, now gift baskets? Still, if she needed them... "I'll get them."

With a sigh, she hugged the box and rested her head against the seat back.

Sterling tucked the sleeping bag around her before closing the door and hurrying back to her car. A quick inspection assured him that Bert and Ernie seemed all right—and unearthed several large gift baskets, a massive bag of dog food and a canvas shopping bag with puppy supplies. With his arms loaded, the dogs led him from her car to his truck. It took him a while, fighting against the sleet and rain and wind every step of the way. Driving conditions were only going to get worse, so the sooner they got to his cabin and off the road, the better.

"Boys?" Cassie whispered as he put his truck into gear.

"Bert and Ernie are in the back seat." He shifted gears and pulled onto the icy road. "And so is all your stuff. Some of those gift baskets might need repacking."

"'kay." She burrowed into her sleeping bag, peering inside the box before covering it with the towel. "Poor little things." Her brow furrowed. "Head hurts."

"You knocked it." He glanced at her. "Anything else hurt?" Could he risk driving back into town? They were on the downward side of one hell of a hill—and they'd have to cross a bridge—to get there. But, if she needed medical attention, he'd go.

"Bruised. That's all." She opened her eyes. "Sterling." She blinked. "This is real?"

"Yeah." He nodded, swallowing hard. "All real."

Her giggle was soft. "You smell the same."

What? He risked another glance her way, struggling to process what that might mean. But his tires slid, and it was just enough to remind him that the only thing that mattered right now was getting to safety.

The dirt and gravel leading to the cabin was

more like an icy mud slick than a road. *Great*. No way was he going to get them stuck and land Cassie stranded again. He kicked on the four-wheel drive and drove along the side of the road to avoid the muck. If the homeowners had a beef with it, he'd pay for damages.

The cabin was more rustic than he'd expected. Smaller, too. But Yvonne knew he wasn't one for bells and whistles, so... The strand of Christmas lights strung along the tiny porch were almost pulled free. They danced and whirled in the wind like a tiny tornado of colored fireflies. At least they had power. That was something.

He parked, left the truck running and punched in the code to open the door. After flipping on a few lights, he placed a log of firewood to brace the door open, and headed back outside.

"Go on inside, boys." The dogs jumped down and ran into the cabin before he opened the front passenger door. "You ready?" He didn't like how pale she looked. Or how still. "Cassie?" The puppies were sounding downright pathetic, but she didn't stir. Considering she'd always had something to say, he couldn't stop the twist in his gut. *Dammit*.

He pulled Cassie into his arms, made sure the puppy box was secure, and carried them all inside. He kicked the log off the door, and the wind slammed it shut with a hard thud. It was easier to sit on the long, overstuffed couch with them in his lap than try to put them down without disturbing someone. There were whimpers coming from the box, but a quick inspection assured him both pups were warm and wiggling.

Cassie, however, was neither. She was cool to the touch and, other than breathing, not moving much at all. From what he could see, the cuts along her hairline and temple were superficial. At least, he hoped that was the case. He rested his hand against her shoulder, and she gasped and pulled away from him. "That hurt?" he whispered. "Cassie?"

"Seat belt." She sounded sleepy. "It worked."

"A fact I'm mighty grateful for." Thinking about what might have happened— Well, the fear that raced up his back turned his blood to ice. She was safe. They were safe. He closed his eyes and took a deep breath, hoping to calm the rapid beat of his heart. He should get his things out of the truck, take stock of the cabin and get a fire started, but he wasn't ready to let her go. Bert and Ernie sat at his feet, their gazes locked on Cassie. "Worried about her, too?"

Bert whimpered, cocking his head to one side.

Ernie put a paw on his knee.

"I'm fine." She blinked, trying to sit up.

"Hold up. You've got a lapful." He carefully placed the puppy box at his side on the couch.

"They okay?" Her gaze darted from the box to him.

"They're just fine." He offered her an attempt at a reassuring smile.

Her smile was slight. "I imagine they'll be hungry soon."

He remembered how much work Bert and Ernie had been when he'd found them. Little tufts of matted fur and pitiful sounds. He and Cassie had fed them every two hours and had loved every minute of it. This wouldn't be like that. And Cassie was in no shape to worry over feeding the pups every two hours. *At least I won't get bored.*

Bert and Ernie whimpered in unison—wanting their momma's full attention.

"I'm fine." The adoration in her voice had both dogs' tails enthusiastically wagging. "I just need a nap." She swayed a bit—placing her hand in the middle of his chest. A few more slow blinks and she was staring at her hand, but she didn't lift it. "Oh. Sorry."

"Dizzy?" He braced his hand against her back.

She tried to nod and stopped, pressing her other hand to her head. "Yes."

He'd had enough concussions to recognize all the symptoms. "I've got some pain relievers in my bag. That should help. That, plenty of water and some sleep, and you'll be feeling better. Though you'll likely have one hell of a headache for a while."

"Awesome." She hadn't moved. One hand pressed to her head, the other resting against his chest—the spot where her gaze remained fixed. "Does that mean we have to move?"

"No." Eventually, he needed to get a good look at her cuts. "Not yet."

"That's a relief." Her blue eyes met his. "What were you doing out and about in this mess?"

He chuckled then. "Getting provisions so I could hunker down until this storm blows over." Not that he'd had much luck. The shelves of Granite Falls Family Grocery were pretty bare by the time he'd thought to stock up. Still, he'd loaded up on beef jerky, a couple packages of frozen macaroni and cheese, a jumbo-size can of nuts, a six-pack of lunch-box fruit salad cups, a few bags of his favorite hard caramel candy, soda pop, and coffee. "You?"

"Heading home." She swayed a bit. "I was programming all the appointment reminders to go out—for the vet clinic. Then those two were dropped off, so I was all caught up in getting what they'd need together and didn't keep an eye on the weather. Obviously." She blinked. "I need... I feel like I'm going to fall over." She sort of crumpled back and into him then, resting her head on his shoulder with a soft groan. "I don't like this."

He didn't like Cassie hurting or feeling bad, but he didn't mind the feeling of her soft body against his. It eased the panic still hovering in the back of his mind. "What can I do?"

"You've done more than enough." She patted his chest. "I don't know what would have happened if you hadn't come along."

He shoved aside the ache in his chest, shoved aside the gut-wrenching fear finding her that way had triggered. Or the fierce bout of protectiveness rising up now, as he stared down at her curled up in his lap. "But I did." The words came out gruffer than he'd intended.

He had no right to feel this way—to feel anything for her. But tonight had been a hell of a night. If he was on edge, he had good reason. It was normal. He could've found someone else and he'd likely have the same reaction. Or close to it. No cause to panic. No big deal. At least, that's what he kept telling himself. "I should probably get everything out of the truck."

"Need help?" She peered up at him.

"Nope." He resisted the urge to smooth her tangled hair from her face. "But I'm going to move you. You want to stay here? Spread out on the couch? Or the recliner? Or the bed?"

"Here," she murmured. "The less movement, the better."

He nodded, lifting her just enough to seat her beside him. "Good?" He stood, adjusting the cushions so she was propped up a bit.

She gave him a wobbly thumbs-up.

"Okay." He stared at her. She was right here, where he could keep an eye on her. "Okay," he repeated.

Bert and Ernie jumped on the couch, wedging themselves on either side of Cassie. The ghost of a smile on her face was enough. Her boys would watch her while he took care of them.

It took three trips to carry in his duffel bag and meager groceries, her squished and worse-for-wear gift baskets, and the bags of dog food and puppy supplies. As soon as his truck was empty, he made a few more trips to lug in some of the firewood stacked along the side of the cabin. A fire was in order. If they lost power, they'd need it. His gaze bounced from Cassie, eyes closed and breathing deep, on the couch, to the abundance of festive decorations covering every inch of the mantel. Candy cane–striped holiday candles and red fleece stockings hung off large brass snow-flake hooks. A miniature Santa's workshop sat in the center, surrounded by glitter-crusted cotton-batting "snow." A strand of colored lights and holly garland had been strung up the wall, across the ceiling, and down the other side. He hesitated, then plugged the strand in. The glow of the pink, blue, yellow, green and white lights was much brighter than he'd expected, so he unplugged it. If she did have a concussion, light might make the headache she had even worse.

He crouched before the stone fireplace and snapped off a few smaller branches for kindling. Before too long, a fire was glowing and popping, and he was holding out his hands for warmth. He glanced over his shoulder at Cassie. No change. Sleeping peacefully, he hoped. That was what she needed.

The puppies' noises, however, weren't going to let her sleep for long.

"Little guys are getting hungry," he whispered to Bert and Ernie. He carried the box into the kitchen and set it on the counter so he could inventory the puppy supplies Cassie had packed. The canvas shopping bag was loaded up with cans of milk replacement, training pads, several small baby bottles and a few small blankets. "Looks like you're all set." He moved as quietly as possible, reading over the directions on the milk replacement before assembling two bottles.

He carried the box and bottles back into the living room and sat in the recliner. "Hungry?" He kept his tone low, wrapping up one of the gray puppies in a blanket Cassie had packed and then holding it close. "It's okay, little fella."

The pup wriggled and whimpered and rooted around until Sterling had the nipple close enough. Then the puppy latched on, grunting and whining.

"Hey, hey, now. Calm down." But Sterling was smiling. The puppy was so small it didn't fill up one hand. "I get that you're hungry." He shook his head. "Careful now or you'll end up breaking the bottle and wearing most of it." He chuckled as the pup pulled fiercely against the nipple.

"I don't think he cares." Cassie's voice was soft but amused. "Poor thing acts like he hasn't eaten in days."

Sterling glanced at Cassie, teasing as he asked, "You've been starving them?"

"You know it." Cassie sighed. "But who knows how long it'd been since they'd eaten before they were brought to me."

"No mom?" Sterling patted the pup's chin and pulled the bottle out of its mouth, triggering a long, pathetic howl from the puppy. "Hey, now, you emptied that whole bottle. You're gonna make it."

The howl continued, so Bert and Ernie hopped

off the couch and sat by the recliner, staring up at Sterling.

"It wasn't me." He finished cleaning up the pup and put it, still protesting, back into the box. "Pretty sure I can't hit that note." He picked up the other pup and a full bottle.

"It's okay, boys." Cassie's tone was soothing. "The man that brought him in said the mom had been hit by a car and was dead on the side of the road. So…"

"You're Mom." He shifted the pup and the bottle until the little thing was nursing comfortably. "They sure are wiggly." He shook his head. "Almost like they're fighting the damn bottle." The pup's gray paws were pushing against his hand while his little mouth tugged against the nipple. "They might be tiny, but they're strong."

"Thank goodness," Cassie murmured.

"I've got this. You rest." He watched her eyes drift closed.

"The fire is nice," she whispered, shifting onto her side and scooching back to lean into the back of the couch. Seconds later, she lifted her arm, and Ernie leapt up. She hugged the dog close against her. "Come on, Bert." She patted the blanket draped over her. Bert jumped up beside her, spun around and flopped against her legs.

It made him smile. Even with a concussion,

bruises and cuts, she was making sure her *boys* were comfy. The gesture, so Cassie, steadied him.

Until he heard her indrawn breath.

"How are you holding up?"

"I'm fine." But she didn't sound fine.

"Cassie…" He tilted the bottle, making sure the little thing got each drop. "You might need medical attention—"

"I mean it." Both eyes popped open.

He cleaned the pup up, put it back in the box and placed the box in his recliner. "Adrenaline is a funny thing." He sat on the coffee table opposite her. "I've seen too many cowboys walk out of the arena and wind up in the ER later. I'm…worried."

"About me?" Her brows rose.

"Of course. Opening that car door and finding you…" He broke off, his throat going tight. It was hard to swallow, but he had to if he was going to get more words out. "It took years off my life." He tried to sound like he was teasing—tried to smile—but he wasn't sure he pulled it off.

Her blue eyes stayed locked with his, but the moment she looked ready to say something, the lights flickered once, then again, before the room went dark.

Chapter Five

Cassie was thankful for the power outage, it saved her from making a fool out of herself. It was bad enough that she was banged up and reliant on him. But for her heart to stutter and stop over his words—to immediately want to ask why he'd left her all those years ago, why he'd been so angry with her... All pointless questions that served no purpose. The past was the past, and that's exactly where it should stay.

She'd banged her head, that's why she wasn't thinking straight. Plus, she'd had a near-death experience. As dramatic as it sounded, that's exactly what would have happened if Sterling hadn't shown up... It wouldn't have taken too much longer to freeze to death. She drew in a wavering breath, glancing up at his dark shape on the coffee table beside her.

She'd focus on how lucky she was. Oh, so lucky. She'd been rescued. Her injuries were minor. She and all the pups were safe and warm.

If the weather wasn't so bad, she'd go but a lottery ticket—straightaway.

"Guess it's a good thing I got the fire going." Sterling stood, his figure outlined by the glow of the flames. "How's your head?"

"I'm not feeling dizzy, so that's an improvement." She'd never had the world around her spinning and flipping and blurry. It had been horrible. Even worse, she couldn't stop it. Hopefully, she was over it. "My head still hurts. Not as sharp as before. More of a steady throb—pressure. If that makes sense? Pushing from the inside of my head. Like it's going to pop…"

"Pretty sure popping heads is bad." He moved into the kitchen, rummaging through something. Seconds later, the soft glow of a lantern cast him in a soft glow "I've got some pain reliever." He returned with a bottle of pills and a water bottle. "Won't hurt to drink that all, too."

She took the two pills he offered and the water bottle. "Thank you."

"Need anything else?" His voice was pitched low.

At the moment, she wanted to sleep, but she knew she couldn't—not yet. "My phone was busted in the wreck. Can I use yours? I should call Buzz."

He held his phone out to her.

"Thank you." She took it and typed in Buzz's number.

"Hello?" Buzz answered on the first ring.

"Buzz? It's me—"

"Dammit, Cassie. I've been calling you." He broke off. "Please tell me everything is okay."

"Yes." She paused. "I know you. I knew you'd be worrying. That's why I'm calling. You can relax now. I'm safe and everything is fine."

There was a pause. "But?" Buzz's voice was tight.

"But I had a minor accident on the way home. The car might be totaled—"

"Sonofabitch. I knew it. I knew something was wrong." He barked, then paused. "She was in an accident." This was muffled, probably telling Jenna. And added, "I am calm," had Cassie smiling. He took a deep breath. "I don't give a *damn* about the car, Cassie. Are *you* okay? And where the hell are you?" He mumbled something, then said, "Where are you?"

"Sterling happened along the road after I'd crashed. Thankfully." She glanced at the hulking shadow by the fire. "I'll stay here until the roads are clear."

Her brother was anything but calm now. "Like hell you will—"

"Buzz Lafferty, stop being an idiot and listen to me." She rarely raised her voice, but now seemed appropriate, "I am too tired and my head hurts too much to yell at you." She took a deep breath. "You have Jenna and the kids to look after. The last thing any of us needs is you out in this mess. Why would you think of putting yourself in harm's way? For nothing? I'm warm and safe and you are too. Let's keep it that way. Stop ranting and think. Please. Listen to me."

Buzz said a handful of colorful words under his breath before asking, "Are you injured? You said your head hurt."

"I'm fine." If she said anything else, Buzz wouldn't stay put and that would lead to even more drama. All she needed was peace and quiet and a nap.

"May I—" Sterling held out his hand "—talk to Buzz?"

Cassie wasn't so sure that was a good idea. "Sterling would like to speak with you. Can you *try* to be nice? Civil, at least? Since he did *rescue* me and all that."

Angrier, muttered words had Cassie wincing before Buzz said, "I can try."

"Gosh, that was convincing." She sighed. "I love you. I love Jenna and the kids. Please stay safe in this mess. I mean it. If you come after me,

I'll never speak to you again." It was a bluff and they both knew it.

"Yeah, yeah." Buzz didn't sound the least bit happy. "I love you, too."

"Good." She held out the phone to Sterling. "He's in a terrific mood."

Sterling's chuckle was low. "Evening, Buzz."

There was a long pause as Buzz undoubtedly said things that weren't civil or nice.

"She's banged up. A few cuts on her head and hand... Uh huh..."

Cassie grabbed his arm and yanked. "Do not say anything about—"

"Pretty sure she has a concussion, too." Sterling caught her hand in his, giving it a gentle squeeze.

She should be angry with him for telling Buzz everything, but she was speechless. At the moment, the only thing registering was his callused fingers holding hers.

"We've got a fire going—" Sterling cleared his throat "—in the *living room*. She and the dogs are settling in for a nap. Pretty much the same thing she'd do with you."

There was a long pause then.

"I know." Sterling's voice was low. "That's not going to happen." He let go of her hand and moved back to the fireplace, his head angled down. "You've got my number now, so you can check in with her."

Cassie groaned at that. "Don't encourage him," she whispered.

But Sterling's posture stiffened at whatever Buzz was saying. "I give you my word," Sterling all but ground out. He stared at the phone, tucked it into his shirt pocket and knelt by the fire to add more logs.

Once upon a time, they could sit quietly for hours on end. Not anymore. The longer the silence stretched on, the more strained the air became. She didn't know what her brother had said to Sterling, but from his rigid posture and silence, it wasn't good. "You're an expert on concussions, now?"

He stared into the fire for a long while. "You could say that."

She'd never heard him sound like that before. Full of anger. Bitterness. Regret. *So much for making things better.* Without meaning to, it appeared she'd struck a nerve.

After he'd left town, she'd catch snippets of conversation about him—football and rodeo were important in small Texas towns. Sterling had shown all sorts of promise during his junior rodeo days here in Granite Falls and folk didn't forget. No matter how hard she'd tried to keep him boxed up and locked away, memories of their time together still resurfaced more often than she'd like.

"How's your head?" He stood, turning to face her. With the fire at his back, his expressions were hidden by shadow.

She patted Ernie as he stretched. "Those pain pills will kick in soon enough."

"You should try to get some sleep." He pointed at the couch. "You comfortable there? With the power out, this is going to be the warmest place in the house." He leaned forward to lift the towel on the puppy box. "They're already sleeping."

"Good. You wore them out, feeding them." She sighed. "I'm comfortable." Ernie and Bert were sprawled over her like a canine lap blanket. "Warm and toasty." She burrowed a hand in Ernie's fur and rubbed Bert's ear. And then winced.

"Your hand?" He moved before she could respond, carrying the battery-operated lantern to the coffee table, and sat to face her. "We should make sure there's no glass stuck. Probably check your head and hair for any slivers." He took her hand in his. "I remember one time, I was on the road heading from a Denver rodeo to Houston. I was with a bunch of guys in a truck that was barely roadworthy and we were dead tired." He held the lantern up, peering closer to inspect her hand. "Joel...no, I think it was Gene...whoever was driving dozed off." His finger traced over one scratch and he shook his head.

She was trying her hardest not to think about how potent his touch was. Or that, this close, his scent wrapped around her like a favorite sweater. "What happened?" She swallowed, her heart doing things she didn't approve of.

"Can you hold this?" He offered her the lantern. "If Bert and Ernie don't mind." But there was a smile in his voice.

She took the lantern with her good hand and held it so he could see. "Better?"

He nodded, his eyes riveted on her hand. "I've got a first aid kit in the truck. It wouldn't hurt to clean these up and put some antibiotic ointment on."

"They're just tiny scratches." She flexed her fingers, trying to stop herself from wincing.

"Cassie Lafferty." He was staring at her face now. "Anyone ever tell you you're stubborn?"

She shook her head.

"Right." He chuckled. "I'm getting the first aid kit. And a comb—so you can brush through your hair." He didn't wait for her to protest. Once he was bundled up, he pulled the door open. The gust of wind that sliced through the fire-warmed cabin was enough to have her and the dogs huddling closer.

"I'm the stubborn one?" She stared at the closed door. "He's one to talk."

The dogs both listened to her, ears perked up and wide-eyed.

"Don't look at me like that." She couldn't be sure, but Bert looked a little disappointed in her. "I know, I know. He's the only reason we're not popsicles right now." She sighed. Saying it out loud made it real. And scary. She'd never been so cold. Wrapping her arms around herself, she whispered, "And I'm thankful for what Sterling did for us."

Bert rested his head on her lap, his tail wagging.

Ernie burrowed under the sleeping bag when Sterling came back inside. "It's getting worse out there." He shook off his coat as he hung it on one of the hooks right beside the front door. "Glad I brought in firewood." Once he'd taken up his seat on the table, he opened the bright red canvas bag he'd carried in.

"So, what happened?" She watched his big, scarred hands dig through the bag.

"When?" He pulled out a small bottle of peroxide, some gauze and a tube of ointment.

"With Joel or Gene? When they fell asleep— driving."

"Oh. I remember now. Gene was driving." He shook his head as he unscrewed the lid on the peroxide bottle. "We crashed." He chuckled. "Wrapped the truck around a tree."

She waited for the punch line. "Really?"

"Yep." He shook his head but kept on chuckling.

"Sounds hilarious." She was horrified. "I'm assuming no one was hurt?" She gasped as he rubbed peroxide over one of the larger cuts.

"We were. Banged up." He blew on her cut. "Glass everywhere. Joel was riding shotgun and his seat belt broke and he went headfirst into the windshield. Lucky for him, he didn't go through it. When he turned around, he looked like something out of a horror movie—his face all covered in blood." He was lightly cleaning her cuts as he spoke. "He says, 'You guys all right?' And we're thinking he's about to fall over, looking the way he did." He pulled out another piece of gauze. "The ER nurse spent a while brushing the glass out of his hair. He had over a hundred pieces in his forehead. None too deep but head wounds bleed like a son of a bitch."

"Poor Joel." He'd painted a pretty gruesome picture. "Were you hurt? I mean, was anyone else injured?"

He glanced up at her before carefully dabbing on more peroxide. "Gene cracked his clavicle. Harvey broke his wrist. I dislocated my jaw. I'd leaned down to pick something off the floorboard and got slammed into the back seat." He reached up to stroke his jaw. "Still clicks now and then." He held her hand even closer, gently running his fingers carefully over tiny lacerations that ran along the outside her wrist and forearm. "I think you're glass-free. And disinfected."

"Thank you." She tried to take her hand back, but he held on.

"Hold up." He held up the tube of ointment. "It's got some pain reliever in it."

She didn't fight as he carefully applied the ointment along the bigger cuts. "There." He sat back, his gaze settling on her temple.

"That bad?" Until now, she hadn't given much thought to her appearance. "Like, Joel-horror-movie bad?"

His grin had her heart twisting and thumping around in her chest. "No. Not *quite* horror-movie bad." He shook his head, his gaze sweeping over her whole face.

The way he studied her didn't do a thing to steady her. It was like he was looking for something. "What?" she asked, her heart lodging in her throat. "What's wrong?"

What was wrong? Every damn thing. Finding her in that car, bloodied and quiet and cold. Injured who knows how badly. They were stuck here without power. And the weather outside showed no signs of improving anytime soon. Now he was so caught up in Cassie, he was staring at her. His memories of her hadn't done her justice. And now... Well, she was so damn beautiful it knocked the breath out of him.

"Nothing." He stood, carrying the gauze to the trash and giving himself some space. It'd taken him years to come to terms with all the damage he'd caused. He'd like to think he'd made amends where he could and, damn it all, he tried every day to be a better man than he was the day before. But with Cassie... Some nights, he still jerked awake with her tear-streaked face haunting him. He'd been so drunk on whiskey and blinded by anger, he'd been out of his head. She'd tried to comfort him and what had he done? Unleashed words so hateful there was no forgetting them—even if she might forgive him.

"Sterling?" Her voice planted him back in the present. "Before we tackle my hair, can we eat?"

"Sure." At least it'd distract him. "I've got some chili. Not the canned stuff, some homemade, bottled stuff I picked up from a hole-in-the-wall diner on my way here."

"Perfect." She sounded tired.

"I'll wake you when it's ready." He saw her

slight nod and decided now was the time to do a more thorough inspection of the house. The owner's rules and instructions for household items were bulleted—straightforward and to the point. This seemed at odds with the overzealous Christmas decorations, but one item on the list caught his eye. They had a gas stove—which would make being snowbound a heck of a lot easier.

He searched the Christmas-bedecked kitchen and unearthed a box of matches, turned on the burner and lit the gas. A bright blue flame encircled the burner and Sterling smiled, humming "Here Comes Santa Claus" softly. A pot from the overhead hanging rack was just the right size for the entire jar of chili. Once it was on the stove, he located bowls and spoons…then stopped. Dishes. Clean up. Water… The pipes. If he didn't drip the pipes, one might break and that would be a whole different kind of problem. If they were really lucky, the water heater was gas, too.

Cassie was dozing, the chili was warming and the puppy box was quiet, so he could, quietly, explore the tiny cabin. There wasn't much to it. Besides the great room they were occupying, there was a master suite and a utility room with the washer and dryer and water heater closet. A peak inside revealed a blue flame. Gas. They were lucky. A working stove and hot water. *Damn lucky.*

After the accident, a warm bath or shower might help with some of Cassie's aches and pains. He'd leave that up to her. Without a fire to keep these rooms warm, it was cold. He dripped the sink and shower faucets and rubbed his hands together.

The master suite was too much. Every inch of the room screamed Christmas. From the large tree in the corner to the snowman candles on the bedside tables. The big bed was piled high with embroidered holiday pillows, a thick Christmas tree–and–redbird comforter, and furry red-white-and-green blanket, which rested on the foot of the bed. There was a large fireplace, too. Pinecones, holly berry branches, candles and a large nutcracker stood at attention on each end of the mantel. From the strands of lights hanging around the room and over the windows, he could only imagine what the place would look like with power. And, in his mind's eye, it wasn't pretty.

Still, she'd likely be more comfortable in here—minus a few dozen throw pillows. But, with their limited stock of firewood, he didn't want to risk it. As much as he'd like to think this would all blow over in a day or two, they needed to be prepared for worst-case scenarios. Besides her life-long love of colorful lipsticks, Cassie was a practical person—she'd understand. He rummaged through the cabinets and closet, finding another comforter and two quilts.

He carried the bedding back into the main room, pulled the door shut behind him and turned to find Bert and Ernie sitting in front of the stove, tails wagging.

"Hungry?" He patted each dog on the head. "Smells good, doesn't it?" He found a set of mixing bowls. "But it's dog food for you two." He filled the large bowl with water and two smaller bowls with food, placing one in front of Bert and the other in front of Ernie. "Eat up."

They did, tails wagging, the crunch of kibble echoing in the silence.

"You two need to keep it down," he murmured.

"Too late." Cassie yawned. "Thanks for feeding them."

"Food is ready." He served up some chili in an elf-and-stocking-print bowl. "But you get chili, not dog food."

"I appreciate that." She chuckled softly.

He filled another bowl, grabbed two spoons and carried everything into the living room. "Here you go." He handed over her bowl and spoon and sat in the recliner beside the couch.

They ate, listening to the snap and pop of the fire and the crunch of the dogs enjoying their dinner. There was nothing left to be done. Other than keeping an eye on Cassie and stoking the fire now and then, he could relax. He tried, but his gaze kept wandering Cassie's way—wondering if he should do more for her scrapes and bruises.

I'm grateful you found her. I owe you… But you shouldn't be taking care of her. Buzz's angry words echoed in Sterling's ears. "You shouldn't be anywhere near her." Which was pretty much what Buzz had said when he'd beaten the shit out of him years ago.

But then Buzz had damn near choked up when Sterling explained Cassie's state, and Sterling couldn't help but feel for the man. He was protecting his sister. At least, he was trying to. Sterling knew how close Cassie and Buzz had been and likely still were. Brother and sister and friends, to boot. They'd grown up in a happy home, with both parents and all the unconditional love and support Sterling had never experienced.

"You're awful quiet." Cassie put her bowl on the coffee table and curled onto her side.

"Thinking." He took a bite of chili.

"About?" Carefully, she leaned against the back of the couch.

Shrugging seemed the best option. His thoughts weren't worth sharing. But she waited, her head turned just enough so that she could look his way. "Nothing much." He finished off his chili, carried their empty bowls into the kitchen and set them in the sink—returning with a comb and towel. "Best lean forward—if you think you can manage it?" He lay the towel on the floor in front of her. "To catch the glass."

Slowly, she shifted forward to sit on the edge of the couch. "I can also manage to comb my own hair." This was said with sass.

He managed not to smile as he handed over the comb. "Lean forward so—"

"I've got this, Sterling." She sighed, leaned forward and began slowly combing through her tangled mop of hair.

He eyed the sparkling shards of glass hitting the towel and frowned. From the looks of it, she'd trapped half the damn window in her long hair. It didn't take long for Cassie's movements to grow unsteady and slow. She was tuckered out but too damn stubborn to ask for help.

She did her best. One long stroke. Then another. Her arm was downright shaking now.

"Can I help?" he asked, returning to his spot on the table to face her.

She sighed, holding out the comb without a word.

He took the comb. "I'll be careful."

"I know." It was a whisper.

It took time. Just when he thought her hair was

glass-free, he'd find more in a knot of curls. She had such thick hair. Thick and soft and gorgeous. He'd loved running his fingers through it. Loved the silky feel of it against his shoulder when he'd held her. Loved the clean, minty scent that clung to each strand. Over and over, he kept on combing. "Hold up." He slid his fingers over her scalp, quick but gentle, until he was satisfied her hair was glass-free.

"You keep that up and I'll fall asleep like this," she murmured, yawning.

"Sleep is what you need." He watched her slump back against the couch. "You sure you're comfortable there?"

She didn't open her eyes as she nodded.

"You need anything?"

She shook her head.

"Then, get some sleep." He leaned forward to fold up the towel.

"Sterling." Her voice was oh-so-soft.

He looked up to find her staring at him. "What's up?"

"Nothing." She blinked. "I just wanted to say… thank you. For everything. I don't know what would have happened if you hadn't turned up…"

Her words conjured up a variety of nightmare-like images. He swallowed against the jagged lump in his throat. "But I did." It was more grumble. "Get some sleep."

"Okay." Her eyes closed, but the tension in her posture didn't ease for some time.

Once he'd cleaned up the kitchen, the puppies were ready to eat. He made up some new bottles, settled himself into the large recliner beside Cassie and pulled out the first puppy.

"I know, I know. You're starving," he murmured. "Lucky for you, I've got that covered." It took some rearranging and patience, but eventually the pup settled on to the bottle. "It'd be easier if you didn't move so much."

The puppy didn't listen.

Sterling shook his head, his gaze sweeping over Cassie—then back again. He couldn't be sure, but he thought he'd seen her smile. Was it because of what he'd said? Or was he dreaming? "We'll never know," he whispered to the puppy.

Since he'd arrived in Granite Falls, nothing had gone the way he'd envisioned. But this, being stuck here with Cassie for who knows how long, was different. *Damn it all.* Other than her injuries, he didn't mind this unexpected development. Not one bit. The truth of the matter was, he was pretty sure he was right where he wanted to be. *Which makes me a damn fool.*

His father had always said Sterling was just like his mother—a desperate, no-talent wannabe who didn't have a lick of sense. In a way, his father was right. For all the insults and abuse he'd rained down on Sterling, Sterling had never stopped trying to gain his father's favor. The more his father withheld it, the harder Sterling tried. It was his father who had plied him with whiskey and planted just enough suspicion to doubt Cassie's loyalty. It was his father who had dragged him from rodeo to rodeo and bar to bar for the next six months. Sterling had paid the bar tabs, but his body was still paying for the foolhardy choices he'd made rodeoing. His heart was, too. Sitting here now, he considered the possibility that his heart had never recovered from losing Cassie. Or, that it ever would.

Chapter Six

Cassie stared up at the beam in the ceiling overhead, testing out her limbs and taking a mental inventory. Her head ached—okay, all of her ached—but it wasn't as bad as she'd expected. She sat up, stretching out her legs and arms and wiggling her fingers and toes, before carefully standing. After spending the night wrapped around Bert and Ernie, it felt good to be up.

The fire had burned down, a few flames casting the room in a dim glow. Last night, she'd been too out of it to take note of her surroundings. All that mattered had been getting out of the cold and finding shelter for her, the dogs and puppies. Sterling had managed to do all three.

Sterling. The man whistle-snoring softly before the fire. From where she stood, the recliner he occupied looked child-sized beneath him. One hand rested on the puppy box at his side, as if he were ready and waiting for the next feeding.

Cassie stooped to peer inside the quiet box right when one puppy stretched fully, his little legs stiffening as far as they could go before his whole body relaxed. The other pup was curled up against its sibling, whimpering softly until the first puppy stopped moving and they could both doze off again. While she'd slept, Sterling had taken care of them.

She turned all her attention back to the man. His feet dangled off the extended footstool of the leather recliner, and his head was tilted back to rest on the top of the chair back. His too-long black hair stuck up in every direction. He looked young—reminding her of a long-ago summer. A good memory. Warm and peaceful and golden. They'd spent the better part of that day swimming around Granite Falls Lake. There'd been nothing like an icy dip in clear water when there were triple-digit daily temps—or the brush of Sterling's fingers along her bare stomach. He'd loved her pink bikini and she'd loved the way he looked at her when she was wearing it. He'd fallen asleep beside her, one arm draping over her and his hand against her side.

For Cassie, that summer had been one of the most magical times of her life.

A roar of the wind outside blew the memory away, but the ache in her heart remained.

He'd come to her rescue last night, but that didn't mean she should go all warm and fuzzy over him. He was attractive, that was a fact. She noticed, also a fact. But she wasn't going to let that cloud her judgment or erase the bitter end to their relationship. How could she?

Bert and Ernie slipped off the couch, trailing after her into the kitchen. The click of their nails on the wood floor made her glance back at Sterling. He was still snoring away.

Good thing he was a heavy sleeper. He needed sleep. Last night hadn't been a picnic for either of them. She might have the scratches and bruises, but he was the one who'd done the rescuing, cleanup and taken care of her and the puppies—all in the middle of a snowstorm.

A snowstorm that's still raging.

Texas was known for unpredictable weather, but this took the cake. A light snowfall, ice on the roadways and a nip in the air was what winter normally looked like. A snowstorm—a blizzard even—was unheard of in these parts. She pulled aside one of the Southwestern-print curtains to peer outside. Sure enough, Sterling's truck was being buffeted with a mix of ice pellets and snow flurries. The strength of the wind only added momentum—the rat-a-tat and clink of ice on the roof was audible whenever there was a lull in the wind.

Bert pushed his nose against her hand, whimpering once.

"You need to go out?" She frowned, the view through the window bleak. "Of course, you do." She gave Bert an absentminded pat on the head. She held up her hand, giving the scratches a once-over. There was no pain or redness, so the ointment seemed to be working.

Both dogs stared up at her, tails wagging.

"It's cold out there, so you better get your business done. And quick." She sighed. "Understand?"

"I think they do." The recliner creaked as Sterling sat up. Running a hand over his face, he yawned, ending on a long, loud groan.

Even though they'd spent the night under the same roof, this was different. She wasn't dazed or confused anymore—she was wary. Cassie tried not to stare as he stood, stretching his arms high over his head so that his shirt pulled up just enough to display a toned back and an angry-looking scar. "I… I didn't mean to wake you."

"I was up about two hours ago. These two don't miss a meal. It's been almost two hours so they'll be sounding off and letting me know it was time to get up anyway." He joined her to peer out between the open curtains. Hands on hips, his expression turned grim. He knocked on the window. "Glad they have double-paned windows." He tugged the curtains apart. "We can leave these open and let in some light."

The day outside was grim, but after he'd opened all the curtains, there was plenty of light to see everything. She scanned the interior, taking in the abundant holiday decorations with a smile. There was no rhyme or reason to the decor and no theme beyond Christmas. As a result, it resembled Santa's workshop—if the elves had gone on strike, thrown decorations all over in rebellion and then added colored strands of lights *everywhere*. She was suddenly grateful there was no power.

"How are you feeling?" He glanced her way.

"A little sore, but fine." Which was sort of true.

"A little?" Clearly, he didn't believe her.

"Much better than last night." Which was the truth.

"These two needing to go out?" He smiled down at the dogs.

Bert and Ernie were all wiggly, their tails and backsides swaying with excitement as Sterling stooped before them.

Traitors. Cassie watched as both dogs circled Sterling, Bert dropping onto his back for a tummy rub while Ernie leaned heavily against Sterling's side. From their enthusiasm, she couldn't stop herself from asking, "Do you have jerky hidden somewhere? They don't normally fall all over themselves for affection like this."

Sterling laughed, patting his shirt front and jean

pockets. "Not that know of." His eyes swiveled up to meet hers. "Maybe they remember me?" His smile faded some and his gaze fell from hers.

She didn't feel much like smiling now either. He'd left them—just like he'd left her—so she hoped they didn't remember him. They hadn't seemed all that bothered, but she'd been so walled in by her own grief she might not have noticed. Petty or not, she needed to be careful about them getting attached only for him to leave. Again.

Sterling cleared his throat. "Or… What's that saying about dogs and babies being the best judge of character?"

Which meant Sterling's character had been completely overhauled or her dogs were just nice to everyone. She was pretty sure it was the latter. Sterling looked familiar and had been nothing but cordial, but it was too early to assume he'd given up drinking. She'd believed she knew him inside and out once, but she couldn't have been more wrong. The Sterling that put his fist through a wall and yelled at her to stop lying to him was nothing like the man she'd loved. This Sterling might as well be a stranger. She needed to remember that.

"I'll take them." Sterling was shrugging into his thick coat. "I need to get something out of the truck and check for more firewood, anyway." He zipped up his coat and tugged on calfskin-leather gloves. "You should take it easy, Cassie. Rest." His gaze darted her way, the muscle in his jaw tightening. "Please."

"I will. You don't need to worry over me anymore." It wasn't exactly subtle, but she hoped he'd get the message. She could take care of herself. Him hovering, *suggesting* what she should do under the guise of concern was a classic Mike move. It set the hair along the back of her neck straight up. She'd let Sterling take the dogs out because her head hurt, she ached all over and he was already going outside. Right then, her stomach growled, long and loud. "After I make us some breakfast." She pressed a hand to her belly. "A girl's got to eat." The sooner she got some food in her, the better.

"No arguments from me." Sterling chuckled and then studied her for a minute, his bright eyes sweeping over the cut at her temple. "If you're sure you're up to it."

"I am." She eyed the bizarre collection of foodstuffs he'd unpacked onto the countertop the night before. "This will be interesting. But I see coffee. We're saved." She reached for the massive can of coffee and patted it on the lid. "I'll start with that."

"No arguments from me." He chuckled. "There's a bunch of stuff in the pantry, too. Read that." He pointed at an envelope on the counter. "We'll be right back."

"Be careful." The roar of the wind was anything but hospitable.

"Always." When he pulled open the front door, a blast of cold wind had the fire sputtering and a whirl of white snowflakes rushing into the main room. "Come on, boys." He waved the dogs out and followed, fighting to pull the door shut behind him.

Cassie shivered, hugging herself. Through the kitchen window, she watched Bert and Ernie do their business a few steps from the porch. Sterling leaned into the wind and headed for his truck.

She pushed off the kitchen counter and found the coffeepot. When Sterling returned, he'd be frozen through. She scooped in the suggested amount, then added another scoop for good measure. Today was a strong-coffee sort of day. She picked up the envelope with Sterling's name on it and pulled out the note—on sugarplum Christmas stationery. "Of course." It wasn't a long note. The owner had left a cheery welcome and gone on to explain the cookie dough, eggnog and a whole variety of holiday treats were for Sterling to enjoy.

"Cookie dough?" She pulled open the refrigerator. "There it is." The homeowners had gone out of their way to stock the place with all things holiday cheer. Eggnog. Stockings full of candy. The makings of s'mores and hot chocolate. Gingerbread and sugar-cookie dough, tubes of icing, and jars of sprinkles to decorate with. "I guess we can bake cookies if things get boring?"

A few minutes later, the door opened and a blast of cold air announced the return of Sterling and both dogs.

"It's colder than a polar bear's pajamas." Sterling leaned against the front door, breathing hard and red-faced.

"I've never heard that one." Cassie poured two cups of coffee and set one on the counter for him. She knelt by the dogs, giving them a quick rub-down with one of the towels she'd found in the bathroom.

"I learned it from Yvonne's kid, Joey. That kid's got buckets of bad sayings." He swiped the dusting of snow from his coat with one hand. "Found some more wood."

Yvonne? The woman he'd been talking to that day at the Frosty King. Were they an item? And Joey. Was Joey his stepson? *None of my business.* "Thanks for taking them out." She nodded at the cup. "Coffee."

"Today's already looking up." He added the wood to the pile along the stone wall before joining her at the counter. He lifted his mug, took a deep sip and sighed with appreciation. "Now, that's what I call coffee." When he took another sip, she could see the crinkles at the corner of his eyes. He was smiling. Over the rim of the mug, his deep, fathomless, dark eyes swept over her.

It's a smile. People smiled at one another. It was no big deal. But the tightening in her chest and the waver of her indrawn breath suggested otherwise. "If it doesn't put some hair on your chest, what's the point in drinking it?" She sipped her coffee, doing her best not to dwell on who Yvonne or how the warmth in his gaze seemed to spread and catch in her stomach. This was bad. This was very bad. After the hate he spewed her way, she couldn't want him. She tore her gaze away, pleased her voice showed no sign of her internal distress. "You two go lie in front of the fire and warm up." She stood, damp towel in hand, and watched as her dogs trotted over to the braided rug before the fire and curled up together.

"You speak dog?" Sterling hung up his coat, tucking his gloves back into the pockets.

"I think we've come to understand one another." He'd been the one to give her Bert and Ernie as two tiny pups *and* told her they were their first babies. For her, it had been a promise of the future they'd have together. *Boy, was I wrong...* "After all, it's been the three of us for some time."

His jaw tightened enough to tell her he hadn't missed her dig.

Right. Instead of continuing her stroll down memory lane, she should find something productive to do. Her stomach sounded off. "So… I'm breaking into a gift basket for breakfast." She eyed the torn decorative plastic wrap and jumbled mess of smashed pastries and crumbling muffins inside. "Technically, one was for the veterinary clinic, so we're not stealing from anyone." She unloaded the treats onto a candy cane–striped platter. "Our hosts appear to take Christmas seriously." As in, everything in the cabin had some Christmas element. "It's everywhere."

He nodded at the mantel. "You noticed, huh? You should see the bedroom."

She glanced at the closed, wreath-adorned door. "Now I know what I'm doing after breakfast." Alone. She needed a little less Sterling crowding in on her.

Halfway through a muffin, Sterling said, "They might not look too nice, but they taste pretty damn good. I could eat a dozen of them."

She believed it, too. Sterling Ford had always been a big man. Tall and broad and intimidating—to those who didn't know him. To her, he'd always been… Sterling. Big, sure. Playful. Strong. And, she'd thought, fiercely loyal. Too bad she'd seen what she wanted to see instead of the truth. She'd believed him when he'd said she was who mattered most and that he could only imagine his future with her at his side. Maybe he'd meant it when he said it and…things changed? Or it was all a lie from the get-go?

Sterling took a sip of coffee, his gaze meeting hers over the rim of his mug.

That was all it took to make her cheeks go hot. She turned her attention to her chocolate croissant.

"Not hungry?" He gestured at her plate with his coffee mug.

It was only then that she realized she'd torn her chocolate croissant into small pieces and arranged them into a circle. "Oh…" She popped a piece into her mouth.

A small crease settled between his dark brows. "What's bothering you, Cassie? Don't deny it, I can tell. You do that. Twist your hair like that."

"Twist my hair?" What was he talking about? She let go of the long strand of hair she'd been toying with.

"You just did it." His brows rose. "I saw you."

"You're seeing things." She smoothed a hand over her hair.

He sighed. "Whatever. Don't believe me, but I know what I'm talking about. You've always done it. That night we snuck out and you had to call your brother to come pull my truck out when the creek flooded? You did that hair-twist thing and Buzz had known you were lying."

"You mean, when you tried to cross, even though I told you not to?" She pushed back. *No. Stop.* She was not going to reminisce with him over one of their long-ago romantic rendezvous.

"You did. I should have listened." His eyes met hers, flashing with something that had her pulse tripping, then picking up speed. "You always told me the truth—"

"Whoa. Sterling." She set her mug down with a little too much force. *No way, no how.* "We might be stranded together but that doesn't mean we need to have some sort of heart-to-heart. If anything, that would turn this already uncomfortable situation into an unbearable one." She took a deep breath, searching for the right words. "I need you to listen, okay?"

Sterling rested his coffee cup on the counter, gripping it with both hands, and held his breath. She had every right to tear him into little pieces and chew him up—just like her damn breakfast. Instead, she was asking him to listen, so he would. It was hard to swallow the lump in his throat, harder still to say, "Okay."

"Whatever happened between us was a long

time ago." She wasn't looking at him—she was tearing the small pieces of croissant into tinier bits, mashing them between her fingertips. "Nothing either of us can say can change what happened."

He nodded.

"We could *not* talk about the past. We could, I don't know, pretend you're a stranger who found me on the side of the road and brought me here." There was a hint of desperation in her voice. "No baggage. No stress. It'd be easier for both us, really, since we are literally stuck here. With no escape." She gestured around the cabin with a shaking hand.

Which was all valid. "I've learned the easy way is rarely the right way, Cassie."

"Is that a no?" She took a deep breath. "No, we're not pretending, we are going to drag it all out and make each other miserable?" She ran her fingers over the cut on her other hand. "Haven't we done that enough? I've spent more than enough time letting thoughts of you make me miserable. You might have done the same."

Except she'd never done a damn thing to make him miserable. He'd been the fool that gave in to a pattern he knew wasn't healthy. He'd made himself miserable. And dammit, she didn't know how heavy his past actions weighed on him. There were times that the self-loathing made it hard to look his reflection in the eye.

Cassie had given him everything—every part of her—and he'd been too blind to see the gift she was. She was one of the few people who knew just how brutal his childhood had been. She'd listened when he'd punched walls and ranted about his father's cruelty and offered him unconditional love and comfort. He hadn't had much of either since they'd parted ways.

"Can't we wait?" He didn't miss the slight tremor in her hands. "At least until we're not stuck here? You might not want to hear some of what I have to say, so I think waiting is a good idea."

He could wait. He'd been waiting. But would she really stop and listen once she was free to go her own way? It might make things uncomfortable, but now seemed like the time to say what needed saying. "I understand, Cassie. But last time I tried this, things didn't go so well. I don't want a repeat performance. We're here, alone, without interruption."

She shot him a *seriously?* kind of look. "So, are we ripping off the damn Band-Aid? That's what you want?" She ran her hands over her face.

"We can ease into it." He shoved his hands into his pockets, his stomach in knots.

She shoved the remainder of her croissant into her mouth. "I'm hungry, remember?" She inspected the slightly smashed pastries before selecting a sausage roll. "I might not be, once we're done talking."

"These are from the new bakery?" He waited for her nod. "How long has Reggie been in Granite Falls?" He sat on the bar stool and watched her take a bite of sausage roll.

"About a year?" She paused, then nodded. "Maybe a little longer."

"Granite Falls has grown since I was here last. In a good way, from what I can tell. That new high school is something." He'd gotten what he wanted and now he was dodging. They both knew it.

Cassie frowned at him. "Well, you've been gone a long time—" She cut herself off. "The town *is* growing, you're right about that. So is the population. The Mitchell brothers are all married with kids. Buzz is engaged. The high school football team made it to district the last three years. And there's talk of the city putting in a splash park down along the river. So, you're all caught up on Granite Falls. Basically, everyone has moved on. Life keeps on moving."

He envied Buzz. And the Mitchells. He'd tried to date, but it never worked. He'd tried, but the only woman he'd ever clicked with was Yvonne. Not romantically, more like the sister he'd never had. Yvonne was a good friend—along with her husband and little boy.

"Jenna was at bingo. Buzz's Jenna." Cassie sipped her coffee, then looked at him. "I guess you weren't introduced?"

He'd forgotten how clear her blue eyes were. "Was she the one keeping Buzz from jumping me at bingo?"

Cassie sighed again, clearly exasperated. "He was not going to jump you." But a crease formed between her arched brows. "I'd like to think he wouldn't, anyway. But then, I didn't know about you visiting or the...altercation you two had." She swallowed, hard. "I'm beginning to think there might be more I didn't know about." Her blue eyes grew intense, searching.

It took everything to keep breathing. This wasn't supposed to be this hard.

"What about you?" She took a sip of her coffee. "What have you been up to?"

"I've been putting a lot of miles on my truck, mostly." He was always on the go, one motel room after another.

Her gaze narrowed the tiniest bit. "*Why* are you putting miles on your truck?"

"Work."

She made an exasperated sound before asking, "Work... Which has something to do with livestock, I hear?" she added, her eyes narrowing a bit. "And rodeo, too?"

"I'm cleared to ride." But since he'd broken his back, the urge to ride was gone.

"I guess that's nice?" She propped her other elbow on the counter and leaned in. "Whoa, whoa, whoa. You really need to slow down because you're overwhelming me with all the information you're sharing." Her brows rose high.

Sterling laughed. Cassie was feeling better. "That's it. You know everything there is to know." He was smiling as he reached for a sausage roll. "I live a pretty uneventful life."

She continued to stare at him, oozing impatience.

"What?" He took a bite.

"You wanted to talk and you said maybe ten words about yourself." She cocked her head to one side, waiting.

"Well, when I'm not on the road going to rodeos or contracting stock animals, I've got a small place in Canyon, Texas. The university up there has a rodeo team and I help out now and then." He paused, not adding he was almost finished with his degree. That was something he was doing for himself. His dad didn't care what he did anymore, Sterling didn't need to prove himself to anyone but himself. If he failed, well, there'd be no one to be disappointed in him. But she was still studying him, so he asked. "Think we've eased into it enough?"

She pulled a strand of hair over her shoulder, twisting it around her finger—making him smile. "I… I guess."

She'd been staring at him long enough that he felt he'd earned the right to do the same. The scratches on her temple. The bruise around them. Not red or inflamed, he noted with relief. Everything else was the same. *Beautiful.*

She blinked rapidly, her cheeks going a soft pink. "You…you said horrible things, Sterling." She pushed off the counter, slid off her stool and started cleaning up.

The anguish in her voice slammed into him. He watched her, his heart thudding so hard in his chest it was a wonder she couldn't hear it. "I was a damn fool."

One eyebrow was arched high. "You were."

"I'd gotten into my head." He tapped his fingers on the kitchen counter. "It wasn't a good place to be. Especially back then."

She looked around the room, avoiding his gaze.

"You want to sit for a bit? Rest?" He paused, holding up his hands. "I'm asking, not telling. I'll make some more coffee, if you like?" He didn't want her overdoing it.

"Okay." She brushed past him to sit on the couch, staring into the fire as she pulled a throw over her legs. "Is your head a better place to be now?" She glanced his way.

Sterling stood and went about making another pot of coffee. "Some days are better than others."

"You didn't say that then. You said it was me. You made me believe it *was* me." She pushed off the couch, wrapped the throw around her and stood, staring at him. "At first, I looked for you. I thought, if I could get you to talk to me, you could tell me what I'd done and I'd change it. I needed you to know I wasn't trying to change you or get in your way."

He rested his head against the kitchen cabinet. She'd done nothing wrong, but he'd let her think otherwise. He turned on the coffeepot and headed into the living room, sick to his stomach. He was a selfish bastard. He'd let her think it was her. Because she believed him.

"Why did you say that? Why did you call me a liar?" Her voice broke.

Sterling was across the room in no time, but she dodged his attempts to reach for her. He stopped moving then, running his fingers through his hair. "Because. Because it didn't make sense for you to want to be with me. Why would you love me?" He shook his head, knowing he sounded pathetic but wanting to be honest.

She stared at him in shock. "I'm supposed to believe this?"

"I hope you will. It's the truth." She had no

reason to believe him, but—fool that he was—he hoped she would. He'd never felt as small and anxious as he was then. waiting for her to say something. Anything. It was almost a relief when the puppy box started to whimper-howl. He wasn't one for baring his soul—unless it was with Cassie. He owed it to her.

The puppies kept howling but Cassie didn't move. Those big blue eyes blinked now and then, but that was it.

"Time to eat." He headed back into the kitchen. "I'll make up the bottles."

Cassie's answer was soft and garbled. "I can feed them."

"Hello, you two floofer-puppies. Aren't you just the sweetest little things?" She picked up the box and placed it on the couch.

Bert and Ernie hopped up beside her to look inside.

"What do you boys think?" Cassie gave each dog a rub on the ear. "These little ones don't have a home. Be gentle and sweet."

Sterling watched her gently pick up one of the puppies and cradle it close.

"I bet Bert and Ernie wouldn't mind being big brothers. Permanently."

Cassie hardly glanced at him when she took the bottle he offered. "Thank you."

He didn't push. They fed the puppies in silence, their grunts and whines and the snap and pop of the fire the only sounds in the small cabin. Even with it storming outside, inside was peaceful. If only he felt as peaceful as the setting. Maybe if she'd said she believed him, he'd feel differently.

Cassie squealed softly. "That's supposed to go in your tum-tum, little one." She giggled.

Sterling paused, his heart thudding over the look on Cassie's face. "Those pups will find no better owner or home than what they have right here." He held up the puppy he'd finished feeding. "She won't listen to me, so you're going to have to tell her."

Cassie looked his way.

"You speak dog, don't you?" He waited.

"I've had a long time to figure Bert and Ernie out." She rubbed her finger along the puppy's nose.

He didn't point out that the storm raging outside would likely give her plenty of time to figure out what these two wanted before the world went back to normal.

Back to normal. She'd be in Granite Falls. He'd be back on the road. Same as before. He'd been doing well for himself. Work kept him focused enough that he didn't worry about things like Christmas decorations, bingo at the community center or the hole in his heart.

His gaze bounced from the storm blustering away outside to Cassie, cooing softly at the tiny puppy she was feeding. This was nice. Too nice. It was a glimpse into what he could have had… and made that damn hole impossible to ignore.

The sooner he got back to work, the better.

Chapter Seven

With the puppies all tucked in for a nap and Sterling rinsing out the bottles in the kitchen, Cassie gave in to her fatigue. Not just her body, but her heart. Sterling's revelation had left her struggling. She knew he'd grown up in a less than loving family, but she'd never considered the scars that had left on Sterling, the man. She didn't know whether to be angry that he'd devalued his worth or sad for believing he'd been unworthy of her love. Either option left a bitter taste in her mouth.

On top of her mental musings, her right shoulder and arm were aching and her head was extra heavy. It didn't take much effort to slide onto her left side and prop up on one of the thick throw pillows. Bert and Ernie stood, resting their heads against the couch cushions, tails wagging. "Hi. I love you, too." She leaned forward to drop kisses on both dogs' heads.

From the kitchen, Sterling asked, "Need anything?"

"Some pain medicine and water, please."

He murmured something under his breath.

"What was that?" She reached down, rubbing a hand along Ernie's side.

"I said okay," he grumbled.

"Why don't I believe you?" She rubbed Bert's downy soft ear.

"Because…" He sighed. "That's not what I said." He stalked across the room with a pill bottle and glass of water. "I said you're stubborn and I let you do too much."

"Let me?" She stared at her hands, the all-too-familiar trickle of unease sliding down her back. "While I appreciate the rescue and everything you've done, Sterling—and I truly do—you don't get to *let me* do anything." She couldn't keep the edge out of her voice.

He studied her before offering her the water. "I only meant…" He ran his fingers through his hair. "I should have offered to clean up and not left it to you—"

"I'm fine." Irritated and achy, but fine.

"No, I sounded like an ass. I'll be more careful with my words." He spoke so softly she couldn't help but look at him.

He was worried. Really, truly worried. The furrow on his brow was sincere. She reached for the pill bottle but almost dropped it when his gaze met hers. There was something more than worry in his warm brown eyes. Her heart stuttered when her fingertips accidentally brushed along his. The contact lasted seconds, but the jolt of it was still rolling over her. Every nerve quivered and hummed. She tore her eyes away, willing her hands to steady as she opened the pill bottle. When her pulse had slowed some, she said, "I'll let you clean up from now on if it makes you feel better." She could feel the weight of his gaze on her but refused to look at him.

He took the pill bottle when she was done and stalked back into the kitchen. She didn't allow herself to stare after him—or let her thoughts dissect her reaction to such a casual touch. Or why her fingertips still tingled.

There were a hundred questions circling in her head, but she was too tired to ask even one of them. She tried to relax. Bert and Ernie had sprawled onto the floor beside the couch, their steady breathing filling the silence. A silence that stretched on and on until she said the first thing that came to mind. "The stockings have glitter on them." She hadn't noticed that before—not that she'd really been paying attention to their surroundings. But now she looked around her with new eyes. "Huh. This place is a...a Christmas cabin."

"Sounds like the title for one of those romantic Christmas television movies they play round the clock." He sat on the other end of the couch, stretching his long legs out in front of him. "Coffee is brewing."

"Sterling Ford watching sweet Christmas romance films?" There was no keeping the surprise from her voice. "That's unexpected."

"No." He shot her a look, then smiled.

Oh, that smile. It rolled over her and left her more twisted up than ever.

"Yvonne does. She records them, too. And she talks about them." He pointed around the cabin and shook his head. "She'd love this place and all this stuff."

Well, that was like getting a bucket of ice water dumped on her head. "Oh." Yvonne again. *Don't ask. Don't ask.* "And Yvonne is…?"

"I work with her." His crooked grin made her heart twist. "She's more than that, though. A real friend. She takes care of me and keeps me on track."

Cassie stared up at the ceiling, his words stirring up a tangle of emotions. After all this time, it didn't make sense for her to feel anything this intensely. And yet…that's what was happening. From the startling shock of his touch to this unexpected pang of hurt over Yvonne, she was feeling all the things. Intensely. *Get a grip.*

"That's nice." Her words were pinched, but they were all she could manage. His profile was all strong, clean lines—except for the scar on the bridge of his nose. Like it'd been broken at some point. His past. A past she hadn't been a part of.

"I'm lucky." He nodded. "I wouldn't know which way was up without her." He turned to face her.

"That's good." She managed to inject a little more enthusiasm this time. He should have someone looking after him. He'd been a loner when he'd stayed in Granite Falls. She'd been it. He'd had lots of acquaintances but no real friends. His cousin hadn't taken an active interest in Sterling when he moved in with him. And when his father showed up in Granite Falls a few years later... She swallowed, glancing at Sterling. His father had terrified her. One look in his eyes and she'd known he wasn't a good person. Seeing him ply Sterling with liquor, then alternate cheering him on and cutting him to the quick only confirmed that. But Sterling had been loyal to a fault, even when his father lashed out. Like Buzz said, Billy Ford was the only constant in Sterling's life.

"You okay?" Sterling's voice startled her from her thoughts.

Was she? "I guess I'm still trying to make sense of it all." She nodded, having a hard time making eye contact when she asked, "How is your cousin, Ricky? Your...father?"

The muscle in his jaw clenched tight. "Both alive." He shrugged. "Ricky is up in Wichita Falls, still welding and drinking too much beer."

She only had the vaguest of memories of his cousin, but that sounded about right.

"My dad… He just gets meaner and meaner." He ran his fingers through his hair. "He lives in Shady Oaks Retirement Home, in Oklahoma. All his hard living caught up with him. I feel for the staff." His gaze darted her way. "It took me too long—and twelve steps—to realize he wasn't good for me. He was a con man. You'd think I'd have seen it but it took a few years to see my old man was always working any angle that would get him ahead."

She tried to smile but couldn't.

"When he showed up in Granite Falls for my graduation, I let my guard down because I wanted him to be this reformed man interested in being my father. I should have known better. I do, now." His dark eyes moved slowly over her face. "I had to learn the hard way and lose everything for my eyes to finally be opened." He took a slow deep breath. "You were at the top of my apology list—and it's one hell of a list."

She swallowed, understanding then. Apologies. Making amends. It was part of the twelve-step program. Back in high school, a friend's mother had gone through the process. It had been hard on the whole family. That was why he wanted to talk through this—so he could apologize.

She was grappling with long-forgotten aches and longings and emotions. Sterling was trying to get a name checked off his list. It made perfect sense, but the pain crushing in on her didn't.

"I am sorry, Cassie. I'm sorry it's taken me this long to say all this." He leaned forward, toward her. "I'm more sorry than you will ever know. I don't expect your forgiveness, but I wanted to apologize all the same."

Her throat was too tight for her to respond. She understood now. All of it. He was shouldering the blame, saying he should have known better than to trust anything his father said or did... But he'd been young and it was his *father*.

"Cassie?" He reached forward, smoothing the hair away from the scratch on her head. "Still hurting?"

"I'm good. No more nursing duties required." She shook her head but didn't lean into his touch, no matter how tempting it was. "But you can check my name off your list."

He was wearing that worried expression again. She was officially too tired to try to figure it out. She yawned and flopped back against the couch. Hopefully, a little sleep would help her figure things out or, at the very least, ease the pain a little. She was dozing off when Sterling spoke up.

"Maybe it's because I haven't decorated for the holidays in years that this seems a little over-the-top. But that could just be me." He stood, poured them each a cup of coffee and carried the mugs back—flicking a strand of bell-heavy garland. "Jingle all the way."

Years? Cassie couldn't imagine. The very idea made her sad. The holidays, especially Christmas, were so special to her and her family. It was a time of tradition and homecoming, love and laughter. Things he'd never had. "I decorate every year and this is way over-the-top." She pointed at the Santa and Mrs. Claus figurines in their toy shop. "I bet those even move when there's power."

He shuddered. "It'd be less creepy if Santa wasn't missing an eye."

"He does look like he's suffered an unfortunate chimney incident." She giggled. "They could have least given him an eye patch. He'd look dashing."

"Dashing?" He glanced at her, that crooked grin back. "Pirate Santa? They should use him for Halloween."

There were those blasted feelings again. Rising up, pressing out from deep inside her. "You could suggest that on the thank-you note you leave for the owner—since they left all those treats for you."

He nodded, looking shamefaced. "I'd feel bad. Especially if ol' one-eyed Santa is special to them. Let's face it, it'd have to be to keep it around." Sterling's chuckle had her smiling his way.

She had always loved it when he'd laughed. It'd been contagious, chasing away the day's trials and making her happy. It'd been so easy. So certain. Just like her love for him.

Sterling yawned, stretching his arms up and over his head. Bert took the opportunity to jump onto Sterling's lap, turn a couple of circles, then fold himself into a sizable black-and-white ball. His sigh of contentment had Ernie jumping up, too.

"Neither one of them realizes they're not lap-dog size." She rubbed Ernie's ear.

Sterling reached over the dogs. "Gotta keep your momma warm, boys." She hadn't realized the dogs had knocked the blanket off her feet, but they had. Now he smoothed it into place and tucked the fabric tight—his big hand resting atop the blanket and her foot.

It was quick and efficient and didn't mean a thing. But all of a sudden, she felt the welling of tears in her eyes and she had no idea why.

As much as she wanted to stop looking at him, it wasn't happening. Amid the chaos of dozens of Christmas knick-knacks, candles and tinsel, Sterling held her attention. The warmth of his brown eyes ignited a fuse she thought she'd stomped out years ago. Boy, had she thought wrong. It wasn't just the smile or his eyes or the rugged handsomeness of his face, it was the electricity between them. Connecting them. Steadily rising. Pulling them close. Setting them on fire. One look from Sterling and she'd known how much he wanted her.

The electricity was just as powerful as ever. And so was the hunger in Sterling's eyes.

It'd been a long time since he'd been tongue-tied. Or sweaty palmed. Or flushed. If he really thought about it, the last time he'd been a bundle of nerves and want had been with Cassie. It could've been the firelight or the quiet intimacy of the space but, damn, she was looking at him like she felt the same.

No. Not just no, but hell no. He wasn't going to ruin things by wanting more. He was practical. Seeing what he wanted to see was anything but practical.

"So…" The word had her and the dogs jumping. He pointed at the games stacked in one of the tinsel-covered bookcases. "How about we break out the checkers?"

She blinked rapidly but nodded.

"Maybe we could take it up a notch and go for chess or—"

"Or we could skip the competitive angle and do a puzzle? It looks like they have one or two or fifty Christmas puzzles on the other shelf." She was far more interested in this suggestion.

He frowned. "A puzzle." But he stood and crossed the room. Anything to distract him from things that could never be with Cassie. He squatted and scanned the boxes, pulling the one with a thousand pieces from the stack. "This looks familiar."

"It does." She smiled. "A snow-covered village."

And damn, but he loved her smile. "I know you love Granite Falls, but I'm not sure it's this picturesque." He cleared off the coffee table and opened the box.

"We'll agree to disagree on that." She slid onto the floor, her blanket secured around her shoulders. "I bet the wind knocked down all the decorations. I don't know if you remember just how seriously Main Street takes the Best Christmas Decoration Contest?" She paused for him to shake his head. "Well, you'd fit right in." She shot him a look. "Poor Dean. This was his first year doing it—after his mother has won the best-decorated shop for the last three years running." She started sifting through the pieces. "Penny Hodges is as sweet as they come. The only exception to that is—"

"—the Christmas Decorating Contest?" He

shrugged. "I'm thinking it won't be everyone's top concern this year. With this storm, folk are likely more worried about any damages or repairs that will need doing." He watched as she picked out all the straight-edged pieces of the puzzle's border and carefully laid them out on the wood tabletop. "Knowing Granite Falls, everyone will pitch in and get things fixed up in no time."

She nodded, snapping three pieces together. "We do look out for each other." She reached across for another piece to add to the border. "What are you doing?" She glanced at his stack of mismatched puzzle pieces.

He eyed his pile, then back at her. "I find pieces and put them together."

Her look was pure exasperation. "It's a thousand pieces, Sterling. You'll never get it done that way." She leaned forward, smoothing out the handful of pieces he'd placed in front of himself. "You could at least sort by color? Or help find all the border pieces. Or pick an image and try to find those pieces... But that might be hard since this is a row of houses. And they all look the same." She shook her head, flipping over his pieces and sighing. "*None* of these match."

She was all worked up. There was a spark in her eyes—he wasn't the only one that was competitive. "Isn't that what we're doing? Finding matches?" He tried not to lean away from her, but she was so close. Too close. And not close enough.

"Yes." She sighed, glancing at him. "But it doesn't have to take the whole day." If she was bothered by his closeness, she didn't show it.

He lifted his hands. "All right, all right. Why don't you show me the right way to put a puzzle together and we'll get it done?"

And she did.

Somewhere along the way, he had to stop listening to her "helpful hints" and focus on keeping his guard up. He was too entranced by the smile that meant she'd found a match or the way her eyes narrowed as she scoured for more. He wasn't sure when she'd started humming "Here Comes Santa Claus" under her breath, but she hummed it over and over again. He didn't want to mention it for fear she'd stop. But the closeness and the song and the stockings and the ridiculous decorations had his mind pulling forward images of past Christmases. Christmases when Sterling was happy to have one gift: Cassie's love.

When he'd said as much to his father, his father had a field day. He'd poked and laughed and belittled Sterling's declaration until Sterling wished he'd kept his mouth shut.

"I always knew you took after your mother but this..." His father had stared up at him, a contemptuous smile on his lips. "She's lived here her whole life, with friends and family, and you think this girl will give everything up for you? You? What the hell do you have to offer her? Life on the road—following you through all your late nights, cheap beer and taking care of whatever aches and pains you get. She gets to watch your dreams get crushed and your anger because life isn't going right for you? 'Cause let's face it, boy, you're never gonna be as good as your old man. When you realize you'll never be the bull rider you want to be, she'll be gone. Time'll come, she'll hate you for taking her away from people that really loved her. People that could take care of her the way you couldn't." His father had been so confident. "She'll leave you, son. You can count on it." He sighed. "If you really care for this girl, you'll leave her behind and save yourself the trouble."

He'd grown up fighting—it was the only way to survive his father's volatility. It'd started with him trying to protect his mother and ended with him trying to protect himself. Fighting over Cassie was surprising only because his father swore he'd turned over a new leaf. And he had—except when it came to Cassie. Now he knew it was because his father needed Sterling to get what his father had wanted and Cassie threatened that. Then, his father's relentless *concern* over Cassie eventually had Sterling buying into his father's manipulations. Sterling had grown up without love, it didn't take much convincing that he was that reason for that. He'd believed he wasn't lovable, plain and simple.

He'd never been so thankful to hear his phone ring—until he saw who was calling. "Buzz." He held the phone out for her. Their last discussion had been more than enough Buzz Lafferty for Sterling.

Cassie took the phone and answered.

From the looks of it, she'd been too focused on assembling the top border of the puzzle to notice his shift in moods or his white-knuckle fists. Instead of eavesdropping on her conversation, he headed into the kitchen and downed a tall glass of cold water. He didn't like where his thoughts had taken him or the unpleasant taste coating his tongue. Even though his father was in a retirement community in Hobart, Oklahoma, there were times his father would point out Sterling's mistakes or laugh at him in his dreams.

"A puzzle." Cassie was more invested in the puzzle than the phone call. "No." She sighed. "Are you serious?... *No.*" Her gaze darted his way.

Was she blushing?

"Everyone good?" She nodded, turning back to the puzzle. "Sure." There was a pause. "Hey, Garrett," then "Uh-huh," and an "Oh, really? Interesting." Whoever Garrett was, she set her puzzle pieces down and leaned back against the couch to stare into the fire. "You'll have to show me. Just the two of us." That last part was whispered. She laughed.

"Hey, Frannie." She nodded. "I know. It looks pretty but you can't play in it yet." She went from nodding to shaking her head. "No, I don't think Biddy should go out and see. She's too little." She paused. "Make sure you go out with Jenna or Buzz. Okay?" Another pause. "Okay, Frannie?" Then she relaxed. "Good girl."

Sterling carried a glass of water to Cassie and sat on the couch. She smiled her thanks his way.

"You better keep an eye on her." He couldn't tell if Cassie was joking or not. "I can just see her opening the door for Biddy. Biddy'd be a snow baby in no time." She sipped her water, listening. "It's fine, Jenna." She took another sip. "Nope. All fine." She was quiet for a long time. "He is a hero. I'd be dead if he hadn't come along and taken me in."

Sterling balked at her frank words.

"He's being ridiculous. Yes, I know. Right." She shook her head. "Buzz didn't believe we were doing a puzzle so… I'll tell him we're having *all* the sex and see if he believes that."

Sterling spit his water out, dousing Bert and Ernie.

Cassie held the phone away from the shriek coming through the speaker. "I should probably wind this up. This is his work phone and I don't want to run down the battery." She paused. "Fine. Put him on." She giggled. "I might behave."

Sterling was still coughing.

"Hi, big brother..." Her words petered off. "You're going to give yourself an aneurysm if you keep stressing out like this. Go stress over the kids. You have teenagers, that's plenty of stress." She sighed, loudly. "No matter what you think, I am an adult. I can do what I like—even if you disapprove. If that happens to be Sterling, so be it." She was scowling now. "I mean it, Buzz. I love you, but whatever is or isn't happening here has nothing to do with you." She pressed the button and handed the phone back to Sterling. "Sorry."

"For...?" He cleared his throat. "Making me spit on your dogs or using me to get your brother all riled up?"

"Why did you spit on the dogs?" She used her blanket to rub the dogs dry.

"I have ears." He shot her a disbelieving look. "You caught me off guard." Now she was smiling, all mischief.

"I might have been a little extreme, but the

point remains that he's way too overprotective. He doesn't trust me to make good decisions." She used air quotes around good decisions. "Like he has to check in on me to make sure there's no nooky going on."

"Nooky?" He'd never heard that one.

"Boinking? Hanky-panky? Knocking boots? Smashing…" She glanced at him again, nodding. "I like to keep up with all the trendy words. I have a teenage niece and nephew, so I need to keep that whole cool-aunt thing going."

"Uh-huh." He had no other answer, but he was getting the point. Buzz was convinced the two of them were going to wind up in bed and Cassie was upset. Not that Buzz was convinced she and Sterling would end up in bed, but because Buzz didn't respect her ability to make her own choices. He wasn't sure if he should be offended on her behalf or wonder if there was a snowball's chance in hell that Buzz should be worried.

Cassie was too worked up to expect a response. She sat a little taller, her tone brittle. "It's offensive, honestly. And it's none of his business. None. He needed reminding. I should have added a little pizzazz but…" She looked back over her shoulder, smiling again. "I've never heard Buzz make those sounds before. I'm not going to lie, it was gratifying."

"Sounds, eh?" He slid back onto the floor and moved around the other side of the table. "Are we talking choking? Wheezing? What?"

"Hmm." She took a sip of her water. "Kind of like an angry chicken. Squawking, mostly. Angry squawking."

He chuckled at the image. "He loves you."

"A little too much sometimes," she grumbled. "It's humiliating to have your brother trying to fix you up all the time. Or, worse, he interrogates anyone I pick."

"I'm not taking his side, Cassie." He tapped a puzzle piece on the table and risked a look at her. "But you're lucky to have someone that cares so much. Irritating or not, he wants only the best for you." *Which doesn't include me.* He touched his nose. "You deserve the best." Which was probably something he shouldn't have said out loud.

Cassie stared at him, her expression blank and her posture more rigid than ever. "What does that mean, *the best*? It's like the word *normal*. *Normal* doesn't really exist. Neither does *the best*. The best man for me would be the one to really, truly love me—irrevocably. A man that would value me and my wants and never take me for granted. And the odds of finding this man, in Granite Falls, is slim to none." She shrugged. "What's the point of setting such high expectations when they'll end in disappointment and heartbreak? Twice was enough. More than enough. I think I'll be just fine with Bert and Ernie and those squirming cuties in the box." She picked up a puzzle piece. "Even Buzz can't argue over that."

But her words sliced through him. Twice? She'd had her heart broken twice? She'd loved the bastard Buzz told him about. It wasn't right. Or fair. What she wanted wasn't too much. It was as it should be.

He'd screwed it up royally the first go-round but he'd been young and so damn stupid. It'd taken cracked vertebra and a punctured lung for him to realize this wasn't about his dream—this was about proving his father wrong. Instead of wasting all that time and energy on chasing belt buckles and big payouts, he should have stayed with Cassie and proven his father wrong that way. Rodeo hadn't been his dream, she was. If he could go back, he'd choose differently. He would love her, value her and her wants, and never take her for granted.

Sitting there, studying her while she sifted puzzle pieces, he suspected he still would—if he was given the chance.

Chapter Eight

She wasn't sure what triggered Sterling, but he was in constant motion for the rest of the day. He took the dogs outside, dug through his truck for anything he'd missed, warmed up leftover chili for their lunch and fed the puppies on his own—asking she take it easy. He also told her he wasn't telling her or ordering her to do anything, which was really sweet. Not that she said as much out loud. He didn't need to know she was thinking about him at all.

Instead, she sprawled on the couch and flipped through a magazine full of holiday recipes. While some of them sounded tempting, nothing could compete with Sterling feeding the puppies. The way he cradled the tiny things in his massive hands and spoke soft words of encouragement was irresistible. As if she needed more to make Sterling irresistible.

Ever since she'd hung up on her brother, her joke had become less and less funny. In fact, her joke had turned into a no-way, that-can't-happen-no-matter-how-much-I-want-it-to sort of scenario. It was an illogical and ridiculous and completely toe-curling idea that had her insides melting. If she wanted a surefire way to crash and burn, this was it. So why was she still thinking about it? Sex. With Sterling. She nibbled on the inside of her lip and let her imagination run wild for a few minutes.

He'd come to apologize and check her name off his list. Done. Now he was free to move on and do…other things. They were stuck here. At one time, they couldn't get enough of each other. Who says they couldn't rekindle some of that heat and enjoy one another? If memory served, there was a whole lot of enjoyment to be had for both of them. Asking him for some nooky wasn't that big of a stretch, was it? She giggled. Nooky. She kept giggling, so she covered her mouth.

Yes, yes it is.

Assuming she could even get the words out. She pressed her eyes shut, but the giggles wouldn't stop. It was nerves. Lots of nerves. She wasn't se rious…was she?

How did one even suggest a one-night stand? Or, weather depending, a several-nights' stand?

Do people talk about it? Discuss details and stuff? Or do they spontaneously sort of…happen? And, if that were the case, was she just supposed to climb into his lap and kiss him? Her lungs contracted even as a fiery warmth flickered to life in her belly.

What am I thinking? She needed to stop—to snap out of it.

"Cassie?" Sterling was giving her the oddest look.

That was when she realized she was wheezing and giggling, with the magazine crumpled up and pressed tight against her chest. "Yes?"

"Something funny?" The corner of his mouth kicked up.

That crooked grin had her sucking in a deep breath. "Yes." She eased her hold on the magazine and smoothed it with her hands. "Hysterical. This article..." The words stuck in her throat.

"Let me see." He reached for it.

"What? Oh no." She wrapped her arms around the magazine. "It's silly. Not that funny."

His eyes narrowed, but he kept on smiling. "Then, why have you been giggling like crazy for the last five minutes?"

"I, well..." She shoved the magazine down between the couch cushions, her face on fire. "It wasn't all about the article."

"Oh?" His expression didn't change. "I'm listening." He rubbed his hands together and sat back, wearing his knee-weakening smile, waiting for her to explain.

Her lungs felt close to bursting. "About…" *Say it.* If he laughs, she could laugh it off—say she was teasing. She opened her mouth. "If you would…? Could we…? Um, can I have a…*bath*?" *I'm such a chicken.* "The water heater is gas, right?" Her face had to be bright red, her cheeks were blazing hot.

"Yeah." He carefully put the puppy down in the nest of blankets and towels in front of the fire. He fluffed up the blankets around them and smiled as Bert and Ernie lay with the mat between them. "You two keep them safe." He gave each dog a head pat.

If he kept being so sweet, she'd tackle him and there'd be no need to say a thing. But if she did that and he wasn't on board, then…would he drop her? She winced. Tackling was out. "They're such good boys." She watched the exchange, her chest deflating.

"I'll get you a bath started, but the rest of the house is pretty cold."

"Oh." She'd been too busy considering all the possible outcomes jumping Sterling might lead to to worry about anything else. "Right." Cold or not, she was still a mess from the accident. Maybe an icy dip would cool her wayward thoughts. "I can take a speed bath."

He chuckled. "I do have a small camping heater,

runs on butane, but I don't know how long it'll last."

"Perfect." She untucked herself from the blankets.

"How about I get the bath set up—"

"No. I'm fine." Whatever twinges and pains she still had had taken a back seat to the ache for him. "I can run a bath for myself." At the very least, a good soak would refresh her and prevent further Sterling ogling.

"Fine." He stood, holding out his hand. "I'll get things warmed up in there first."

Sterling had no idea. She couldn't remember the last time she felt this…warm. She was feeling all kinds of warm. He was waiting for her to take his hand and she was fighting the sudden urge to giggle again. More giggling would be bad.

"I'm only trying to help. Offering it, that is." He was not the least amused. "I'm not suggesting you *need* help. Or that you're not capable of getting up on your own—"

"No. I… I appreciate it." She took his hand and let him pull her up. "Thank you." And then she hugged him. "For everything." Why was she hugging him? Why did he smell so good?

His arms went around her. It was a loose embrace, nothing special. "No thanks needed."

She wanted him to pull her closer. "You're wrong." There was too much space between them.

His chuckle rolled out of him—husky and deep and oh-so-inviting. "I knew you were going to say that." He stared down at her. "That was one of your favorite things to say to me." His smile slowly dimmed and the muscle in his jaw clenched tight.

Was he angry? Or was he longing for her the way she ached for him?

She took a deep breath and stepped forward. No room between them now. Just him, staring at her, and her, willing him to do what she was too nervous to do. One step. One tug. It wouldn't take much effort for his lips to claim hers.

His arms slid free and he stepped back. "I'll get the heater going." He swiveled on his heel and disappeared through the bedroom's door.

Disappointed slammed into her. Then embarrassment. She wasn't one to put herself out there on the dating scene, but there was no misunderstanding his response. *No, thank you.*

Okay. That just made all her hemming and hawing over to jump him or not to jump irrelevant. He doesn't want to be jumped—not by her. Thank goodness she hadn't thrown herself at him. That would have made it ten times more awkward. It would have been awful. Humiliation galore.

She took a deep breath and let that sink in. The mortification was one thing, the hurt was something else. Better to let it go and move on. No hurting or sadness and absolutely no tears. She took another deep breath and stiffened her spine.

It was something. Now she knew where he stood. She could stop thinking or feeling or wondering. Take a bath and get a grip. Afterward, she'd be her rational self and there'd be no more inappropriate Sterling thoughts. *Here's hoping.*

She joined him in the bedroom. "You weren't kidding." The cold in the room was bracing. If the living room and kitchen had a decorating theme it would be "Christmas Chaos." The bedroom? "A Garish Christmas Nightmare"? She hurried to the bathroom, thankful for the blanket she was bundled into. "I don't know if the owners hired a decorator, but if they did, the decorator needs to be fired." She pulled the bathroom door shut, rubbing her hands up and down her arms and crouching in front of the tiny heater. "And have their decorator license taken away. If that's a thing? If not, it should be. It might prevent rooms like that from happening." She grimaced.

"I told you it's bad. No idea about the license thing, but I'm thinking *no* professional would come up with that." He'd already turned on the water and reached to test the temperature. "Maybe they'd had a little too much eggnog before they started?"

She sat on the floor, tugging her blanket tight and holding her hands out to the heater. "That would explain it."

"Eggnog might help warm you up from the inside?" He watched her rubbing her hands together and smiled. "Though the water's good to go. Might be on the hot side."

"I'll take it." She stood, dropping the blanket and tugging off her socks. "You better run because I'm getting in."

"I'm going." And he did, the door slamming behind him.

She laughed, tearing off her clothes and stepping into the bathtub. "Perfect." She sighed, relaxing after a few seconds. The bathroom was decorated, too, of course. Bathmats, towels, candles and two oversize and mega fluffy holiday bathrobes hung from the back of the door. Either they were expecting abominable snowmen or the homeowners were giants.

A bright green basket held a collection of guest soaps and bath gel. "Christmas cheer everywhere. Peppermint? Or gingerbread?" At this point, she should expect nothing less.

The gingerbread smelled horrible, but the peppermint was light and minty fresh. She lathered up the red-and-white-striped bath sponge and scrubbed all over. It was heavenly. She hadn't realized just how grimy she felt until now. She had been in the same clothes…

Her clothes. The pile of dirty clothing lay on the holly-covered bathmat. "Crap." It's not like she drove around with extra clothes in her car.

But, all lack of taste aside, their hosts had provided a clean alternative. "Looks like I'm going to embrace my inner yeti." The massive, fluffy blue robe, covered in white snowflakes, would likely engulf her. It wasn't exactly clothing, but it would do until she managed to wash hers.

When her hair was peppermint fresh and her skin was getting goose-bumpy, she made a dash for one of the thick towels and dried off as quickly as possible. She shoved her dirty clothes into the washer, wrapped her hair in the towel, slid on the massive robe, grabbed handfuls of extra fabric so she wouldn't trip and ran back into the living room. "Your turn." She tugged the door closed and shoved her hands into the robe's pockets. "It was great—until I got out. Now I'm really, really cold."

The dogs had been lying on either side of the puppies' nest, but they both jumped up and started barking at her.

"It's me." She held up her hands, pushing the too-long sleeves back. "Just me."

Bert whimpered and Ernie's tail started wagging, but they didn't look totally convinced.

"I'm gonna side with them. I might need convincing it's you." Sterling cocked his head to one side. "What the hell are you wearing?"

"A nice, comfy, fluffy—"

"You can't miss the fluffy." He gave her a head-to-toe inspection. "Or that it's three sizes too big."

She curtseyed—and nearly tripped over the extra fabric. "Hey, I'm thankful. Better than putting back on my dirty clothes. When we get power back, I'll probably run them through the washing machine twice." She reached up to the towel around her hair. "Can I borrow that comb again?"

He nodded. "In my bag, in the small bag. Help yourself." He reached for the fire poker and shifted the logs to make space for another.

His bag was surprisingly tidy. Jeans rolled up. Shirts folded. Socks and boxers. She pushed those aside and there was his toiletries bag. While she was tempted to inspect the contents, her toes were getting icy. She grabbed the bag and carried it back to the fire. She sat next to Bert and tucked her robe in around her before unzipping the bag. Toothbrush and toothpaste, a razor and some shaving gel. And the comb—right next to his cologne. The scent floated up, instantly conjuring up new images of her and Sterling, scantily clad, and tangled up in each other. The odds of that happening were drastically diminished now that she was dressed like an abominable snowman. She swallowed again and grabbed the comb.

"Find it?" he asked, sitting on the table, and patting Ernie's side.

"Yep. I did." She held up the comb. "Right here." She zipped up the bag and set it on the table. Even as she ran the comb through her hair, his scent tickled her nose. Beneath her abominable-snowman getup, she was feeling all sorts of tingles and stomach flutters. "It's good you have everything—your things. I mean, it makes sense with you being on the road a lot." She kept combing, hoping the fire would dry her hair. "You won't have to wear the Santa robe in there."

"Who says I don't want to wear the Santa robe?" he teased, his eyebrows high.

"Far be it for me to stop you." She glanced at him. "I'm sure you could pull it off." Sterling, naked, in a Santa robe? That was alarmingly exciting. If she could goad him into the hooded snowman robe, she would. "Too bad we'll never know."

"We won't?" He stood, both dogs eyeing her warily.

"Bert." She cooed. "Ernie." They sniffed the hands she offered. "It's just your mom. Do I smell funny?" They both leaned into her hands, then curled up against her sides. "Steer clear of the gingerbread bodywash."

"I like gingerbread."

"Okay." She hugged the dogs. "Suit yourself. But don't expect me to cuddle up with you if we run out of firewood." She wrinkled up her nose and shook her head.

"I've been warned." He grinned and held out his hand. "I'll hang your towel in the bathroom."

"Thank you." She handed over the wet towel. "I'd do it, but I think I'm trapped for the moment." Bert grunted and stared up at her with adoring eyes, while Ernie rolled over and offered up his stomach for rubbing. "You two are the biggest babies." She gave both dogs a kiss on the nose. "And I love you dearly."

"Looks pretty mutual." He chuckled. "If those two are going to get in the way, I can help with your hair."

Her gaze got tangled up in his and she panicked. He was so close. It wasn't his fault that she was struggling. It's not like he could stop being the most handsome-and-sexy man she'd ever laid eyes on. Or that he looked even more so bathed in firelight. Or that watching him be so tender with the puppies tugged at her heart... When he brushed the glass from her hair or helped her up, he'd no idea that his touch stirred her. He was being kind.

And it frustrated her. While she was stealing hidden glances of his manly beauty and fantasizing about him in a fluffy Santa robe, he was feeding puppies and offering to brush her hair. What she really wanted was to be pressed up against the wall with Sterling pressed against her. That's all she wanted. So much. None of this was his fault—he probably was oblivious to her feelings. That's why she was so frustrated. That's why she all but spit a single word at him. "No."

He was pretty sure that *no* applied to a hell of a lot more than him brushing her hair. Whatever she'd been thinking, it'd built and grown until she'd looked ready to pop. And she had. That *no* erupted from her with enough force to have him step back. Even the dogs were sitting up, regarding her with wide eyes.

"I'm tired," she whispered, wrapping her arms around her knees to rest her chin. "I'm sorry."

It was a blatant dodge, but he should let it be and give her some space. Her head was the only visible part of Cassie in her massive robe cocoon and she looked so small and vulnerable that he couldn't.

"You're sure that's all it is?" He hated not knowing what she was thinking. He'd no way to make it better. And, damn it all, he wanted to make it better—if he could. "We're gonna be stuck here for a few more days, Cassie. Whatever's eating at you, I'm game to listen."

Her sigh was long and loud and bone-deep. But it wasn't an outright no, so he sat opposite her on the edge of the coffee table and waited.

"Some things are best left unspoken." She waved her hand—rather the arm of the too-big robe swung back and forth.

"Not if they're twisting up your guts. Believe me, Cassie. I had to learn that one the hard way." He wanted to reach for her hand.

She lifted her head and looked at him.

"We could take turns." He shrugged. "I've got plenty to work through. Maybe we can help each other out? Let off some steam?"

She nibbled on the inside of her lip, her gaze narrowing just a bit.

"I'll shower and you can think it over." He stood. "No pressure."

She continued to study him but didn't say a word.

"You boys keep an eye on her. Help her brush her hair if she needs it." He grinned, hoping to ease some of the tension. Before he closed the bedroom door, he thought he saw a ghost of a smile on her lips.

One whiff of the gingerbread bath gel and he

was screwing the lid back on tight. Cassie had warned him. Whatever that smell was, it wasn't gingerbread. Peppermint wasn't his thing, but the scent was refreshing and clean. He scrubbed and rinsed and scrubbed again, giving her some time to consider his offer.

He turned off the faucets when the bathroom was foggy and warm. Yeah, he had clothes to wear, but that robe might be just the thing to relax Cassie. Once he was dry, he pulled on the Santa robe and ran his fingers through his hair. There was no making this look better but it was soft and thick. He might look like a damn fool, but he was warm.

When he stepped into the living room, he paused. "What do you think?" He spun slowly, for effect. "Can I pull it off?"

"I've never wanted my phone more than I do right this minute." Cassie covered her mouth, but he could hear her laughing.

"Because I look so good?" He struck a pose, winking at her. "I know it."

She was still laughing when she threw a couch pillow at him.

He caught it right before it smacked him in the face. "Good aim." He rubbed his hands together. "You want some eggnog?"

"Dressed like this, I do feel a sense of obligation." She stood and followed him into the kitchen, the dogs trailing after them.

"Coming right up." He pulled the eggnog from the refrigerator.

"Cups." She eyed the stemware. "Do you want penguins or redbirds?"

"I'm a penguin man, myself." He nodded at his selection.

"You are?" Cassie slid the glasses closer to him. She didn't say anything when he filled his glass with water.

"Cheers." He held out his glass. "To gas stoves and water heaters."

"I'll drink to that." She touched her glass to his and took a sip. "Oh my." Her whole face scrunched up. "There's a lot of alcohol in there."

He sniffed the jug of eggnog. "Yes, there is." He saw the way she glanced at his glass again. "I've been sober for three years and a couple of months."

"Good for you." Her smile trembled a little.

It gutted him that his drinking had affected her. "I didn't like who I was when I was drinking."

She opened her mouth, then closed it.

"Go on." He wanted to know what she was thinking.

"I think maybe we could try this whole back-

and-forth thing you suggested?" She sipped her eggnog. "If you're sure that's what you want?"

He was so damn relieved she was taking him up on his offer. "Yes, ma'am." He took another sip of his water.

"It might be the eggnog talking, but you do make that robe work." She smiled, her gaze sweeping over him.

"Good. If things ever get really dire, I could play a mall Santa." He liked the way she laughed, he always had. There'd been times her laugh was the only thing that could lift his spirits.

Bert whimpered, resting his paw on Cassie's foot. "Did you think I'd forgotten your dinner?"

"I'll feed them and take them out if you want to get bottles ready?"

"You're not going outside like that?" She stared at him, wide-eyed.

"It won't take long." He shrugged. "We won't be out there long enough to freeze anything important off."

"I'm going to want clarification on that. Hurry up." She was laughing all over again. "I'll get the bottles."

He regretted the offer the moment he stepped outside. He'd stepped into his cowboy boots, but they didn't do a thing to keep out the cold. And the robe? Well, it wasn't made for outdoor wear—

especially when it was below freezing. "Hurry up, boys." He shifted back and forth, from foot to foot.

"You're looking a little blue." Cassie was waiting for him when he came back inside. "Nothing fell off?"

"Nope." He grinned. "Nice to know you were concerned."

She rolled her eyes and carried her eggnog and the puppies' bottles back toward the fire.

He kicked off his boots and fed Bert and Ernie before heading for the fire to warm his hands. "It's damn cold out there."

Cassie piled all the couch pillows onto the thick braided rug and lay on her side. Bert and Ernie were all too happy to occupy the space along her back. "I'm ready."

He wasn't sure what she was ready for, but he couldn't complain about the view. Cassie was beautiful no matter what. Cassie in firelight was... Well, she damn near took his breath away. Her long hair was spread over one pillow. She reached over to lightly rest her hand on one puppy, then the other. The movement was enough to shift her massive robe just enough to reveal her collarbone. A collarbone he'd kissed and nuzzled.

"Are you?" She glanced up at him. "Who's going first?"

He sat on the other side of the puppies, stretching his long legs out and reclining against the stone hearth. "You pick."

"Easy." She propped herself up on one elbow and sipped her eggnog. "You."

She had no idea how sexy she was. For the first time, he was grateful for the abundant fabric of his robe. With any luck, it would hide the evidence of his mounting arousal. "Okay." He took a long sip of his cold water. "I'm here to work with the McCarrick brothers, to check out their stock and see if we want to sign them on as a regular supplier for cutting horses."

She nodded.

"I pride myself on being professional. I've spent the last three years busting my ass to get ahead and earn some respect, get a handle on my drinking and try to make peace with my past. Then I see the McCarrick brothers and I know I've got the power to change their future. Or not. I'm struggling with that."

"What did they do?" She set aside her empty glass. "I get the feeling there is a history there or some reason you're not sold on signing them. As men, they're too loud and hotheaded and more than a little opinionated. But they know horses. They don't mess around when it comes to their ranch."

"You're saying they'll do right by the rodeo company?" That was all that should matter.

"I am." She nodded. "But you should talk to them, Sterling. I won't push for details, but I'd think it'll be hard to work with someone if you've got an axe to grind."

He nodded. "Yvonne said pretty much the same thing." She was the only person he'd told about his last visit to Granite Falls.

"Yvonne." Her tone was brittle. "Sounds like she's got a good head on her shoulders." She sat up, her robe parting a little farther. "My turn?"

He nodded, keeping his eyes glued on her face.

"My brother is trying to fix me up with a nice guy." She took a deep breath and frowned at her empty glass. "And he is a nice guy."

"Nice guys are good." Who was this nice guy?

"But he doesn't..." She shook her head, her long hair bouncing. "There's no spark. None. I wish there was. It would be so easy then."

"You think it could develop? In time?" He watched a furrow crease her forehead.

"No." She met his gaze. "I don't want to hurt him. I have tried to tell him the truth, but he's quite determined. He thinks our friendship will lead to something...more." She blew a curl from her face. "And maybe he's right. But I think I'd know what was missing. I'd feel that...void. I'd feel bad for that, for him, if I never reciprocated. No one should settle if there's even the slightest chance at real love or passion. Or does that just sound weird?" She smiled as one of the puppies squeaked. "That's why being a dog lady just makes sense."

"It's not weird. The dog-lady thing is, but I get what you're saying about settling." He paused, choosing his words with care. "Tell whoever it is—"

"Dean. Dean Hodges." She glanced at him.

"Dean." Dean Hodges was Buzz's choice? Dean? He was a nice guy but, well, he was a nice guy. After seeing his sister broken by two different men, it made perfect sense for Buzz to want a nice guy for Cassie. Dean was steady. Reliable. Gentle. Cassie deserved all those things.

"What's that look mean?" She seemed nervous. At the very least, uncomfortable.

"Nothing." He tried a casual shrug. "Thinking about Dean and you." And he didn't like it.

"I can't even kiss him. I tried once and I ended up laughing."

Good. "That's a pretty strong reaction. You're going to have to go with your gut on this one. This is your life, so live it."

"There is this other guy." She rested her chin on her knees again, those eyes searching his. "And he makes me feel all the things Dean doesn't."

Each word cut through him. There was someone else. Someone who made her feel things. He didn't want to hear this.

"I don't know how he feels. Does he want me or does he want to get away from me?" Her gaze never left his face. "What if I'm seeing what I want to see?"

"Then, tell him." *Shut up. Shut up.* "If he is what you want, tell him." He ground the words out, hating himself. He tore his gaze away, swallowing against the jagged lump in his throat.

"I don't think I can." Her voice wavered.

He took several deep breaths before he responded. "What's stopping you?"

"Fear." The word was so raw he had no choice but to look at her. "I had my heart broken. You were here for the first one..." She shook her head. "The guy I hoped would help me move on turned out to be a really not-so-nice guy. I stayed, thinking I could change enough to make him happy— since I didn't get that chance the first time around. But I couldn't. He didn't take it too well when I broke it off." She shuddered. "But that was that. Buzz gives me flowers every year on the anniversary of the day I ended it." She hurried on. "That's two strikes." She forced a smile. "Maybe the smart thing is to protect my heart. I could, you know, sleep with this guy—keep it casual? But I don't know how to do that. Is there a conversation to get things started? Is it some spontaneous mutual understanding? I don't know where to begin. Or what to do when he tells me no." She covered her face with her hands. "It'd be a disaster."

He had no words. If it wasn't Cassie saying this, he'd laugh. But it was Cassie. And there wasn't anything funny about this.

"I can't look at you right now." Her face was still covered.

He was having a hell of a hard time looking at her. Not because of what she'd said but of all that she'd revealed. He might be jealous as hell that she was attracted enough to some guy to consider a hookup, but that it was his fault. He and the jerk who had come after him had scarred her so badly that she was taking her heart out of the equation.

"Can you say something, please?" She peeked between her fingers.

"First, I'm just processing all you've said. It's a lot." He worked to keep his voice low and steady.

"Let's forget it." She buried her face in her knees. "I guess the eggnog kicked in. I don't... I shouldn't. This was a bad idea."

He was up and moving to her side then, shooing the dogs aside so he could take their place. His hands clasped her wrists. "No. It wasn't a bad idea." He gently pulled her hands away. "I was surprised by some of what you said—"

"What part?" She cut in.

This close, it wouldn't take much to pull her into his arms. If she needed comforting, that's just what he'd do. "Well, the heartbreaks. I'd like to beat both the bastards to a bloody pulp."

She smiled. "Both of them?"

"Both of them. The first one sounds like a fool. I'm sure he lives every day with regret." He swallowed, hard, and went on. "The second one needs an ass-whupping and then some."

Her breath hitched and, damn it all, tears formed in the corner of her eyes.

"This other thing? This *guy* you want." He wasn't sure what to say. "You don't need to worry. Any man would want you, Cassie." Didn't she know that? "You might as well settle for Dean if you're not going after what you want. You deserve a someone who will love, cherish and want you."

"I'd settle for *want*." Her words were a near whisper.

It went against everything he wanted for her. "If that's enough to make you happy, then tell him. I guarantee he won't turn you down." And the mere thought of it was a knife to the heart.

"Guarantee?" She sat up a little straighter. "You're certain?"

He nodded. Hell, yes, he was certain.

"Okay." She nodded, staring down at his hands

still holding her wrists. "I want to sleep with you, Sterling Ford. I want to have incredible sex with you—lots of sex. No strings attached. No expectations. And when the snow stops, life goes back to normal." She looked up at him, her eyes blazing. "But I want you."

Chapter Nine

*O*migod. *Omigod.* She'd said it. All of it. And now he was staring at her in complete and utter shock. Not exactly how she'd hoped he'd react. Not exactly encouraging either. Any minute he'd say something… Any minute. All the while, his face was a constant shift of emotion.

When she tried to pull her hands away, his hold tightened.

"Is this the eggnog talking? Or is this you?" His voice was gruff.

"It's me." She swallowed, bracing herself. "Making a complete and total ass of my—"

He pressed a finger to her lips. "I just wanted to make sure you're not going to regret this in the morning."

His words stoked the simmer in her belly into a roaring fire. "It's me."

He studied her so long her stomach dropped and her pulse was reaching a rate that was anything but normal. And then he scooped her up and into his lap. His nose brushed along hers. "Let it snow, let it snow, let it snow." His lips brushed against hers, gently. Then again. "Damn."

She was smiling when his mouth sealed to hers. Smiling and gasping and gripping handfuls of his fuzzy robe. Her hands slid up his neck and into his hair to hold him in place. Here, where he belonged, kissing her. It was just the same. Raw and consuming. Only his kiss did this. It was his touch that teased her body to life and gave her true pleasure. This was all she wanted...

Until one of the puppies let out a long, whimpering howl. A howl that Bert and Ernie picked up and carried on—supporting the tiny pup's plea for food.

"Talk about timing." His arms eased, but he didn't let her go.

"Hold that thought." She pressed a kiss to each cheek and the tip of his nose before sliding from his lap. "Poor little babies," she cooed. "And good boys for speaking up." She patted Bert and Ernie. "Don't worry. We'll take care of them."

Sterling sighed, adjusting his robe and drawing attention to the evidence that assured her he was just as hungry for her as she was for him. He noticed, glancing from the rise in his robe, to her.

Just like that, she was blushing. "Which one would you like?" Both pups were tiny, but the one making all the noise was a smidge bigger.

"I'll take the howler." He lifted the squalling puppy and reached for a bottle. "You two need to learn to do this." He was talking to Bert and Ernie.

She laughed. "That would be something."

"I'm not teasing." The look he shot her set her cheeks on fire. "I'm inclined to make the most of our time."

She cradled the other puppy against her chest. "He's a sweet talker, isn't he?" The puppy rooted and pressed against the robe. "Sorry, little one. All I can give you is a bottle." She rubbed a finger over his head and pressed the bottle forward. The pup attacked it. "You're getting the hang of it. Soon you'll have your eyes open and you'll be a roly-poly pup chasing after your big brothers."

"You two hear that?" He was talking to Bert and Ernie again. "That's a big job. A job that includes feeding your little brothers."

She laughed again. "Their lack of opposable thumbs might make that problematic." She was pretty sure the puppies had never taken this long to eat before. It was possible the way Sterling was devouring her with his eyes influenced that. She loved how the air sparked and throbbed between them. He did want her. And as good as the anticipation felt, she couldn't wait to kiss him again. When her attention had wandered to his mouth, she didn't know. Now she had no interest in looking away. Kissing Sterling had always set her on fire.

"Cassie." Her name was a low growl.

"Sterling." She was breathless when her eyes met his.

He shook his head, the fire in his gaze warming every inch of her.

By the time the puppies were fed and they were cleaned up and lazily squirming on their blankets, Cassie was seriously reconsidering her jumping-Sterling plan. But Sterling had them sitting on the couch before she'd had the chance to act.

"Warm enough?" he asked, smoothing her hair back.

She placed his hand on her collar bone. "Very."

He traced his finger along her skin, seemingly enthralled.

She arched into his featherlight touch. "Kiss me?"

It wasn't the gentle brush of his lips she'd expected, it was so much better. His kiss was hungry and impatient. She held on to him until she was gasping for air. The stroke of his tongue drew a moan from her. When her tongue matched his, the rasp of his breath sent a thrill down her spine. Her memories hadn't preserved the force of this. But now that she was wrapped up in his scent and touch and kiss, she gave in to it, to him.

He pulled away suddenly. "Are you cold?"

"No. Cold is the exact opposite of how I'm feeling." She was panting as she smiled up at him.

"You shivered." He was just as breathless.

"That was all you." She slid a hand beneath his robe to rest over his pounding heart.

"That's all you." He smiled before he bent forward to kiss the scrape at her temple.

She loved the way he responded to her touch. When she tugged his robe apart to explore the contours of his chest, his moan emboldened her to do more. Her nails raked along his back, then stilled. His scar. She ran her fingers along the five-inch gash. Whatever had happened, it'd left its mark upon him. What or who had done this to him? She'd find out. Later.

He trailed kisses along her cheek to her ear, nipped along the shell and sucked her earlobe into the heat of his mouth.

She gasped, arching her neck back for more.

He obliged, taking his time navigating his way down her neck. Teeth, lips and tongue—he had her clinging to his robe.

She gave in to instinct, driven by need and nothing else. That was how his robe was untied. It didn't take long for it to land on the floor. Nothing could compare to the feeling of his lips on her neck.

Wrong.

His hands untied the sash on her robe and gently tugged it open. This. Nothing compared to this. Skin to skin, mouth to mouth. She willingly lost herself to the heat of his breath and the slide of his hands on her body. So, when he groaned and stopped moving, her entire body protested.

"You're sure about this?" He lifted his head to stare down at her.

She was so dazed it took a minute for his question to register. "I am. But if you're not—"

"I will always want you, Cassie."

She slid her hands up his chest to twine around his neck. "Well...you have me." She arched into him, her nipples skimming against his chest.

His breath ended on a moan. "Not yet." His hand traveled along her side and along the curve of her hip.

She knew what he wanted, she wanted it, too. Needed it. There was time to go slow and savor each kiss and touch. But, for now, neither one of them wanted to wait. Her heart was pounding as she hooked one leg around his waist.

He thrust once, twice, then buried himself inside of her—his groan long and broken. His lips latched on to one nipple, teasing it until she'd was arching into him. He started to move then, a slow, steady rhythm that had her moaning with pleasure.

Over and over, faster and faster, they came together again and again. She clung to him, pressing kisses to his collarbone and neck. She pressed her nose to the center of his chest and she was done. His scent flooded her and tipped her over the edge. He caught the cry of her release with his kiss, thrusting hard against her until he climaxed.

Cassie cradled his head against her chest, her fingers sliding through his thick hair as their ragged breathing filled the air.

"Am I crushing you?"

"Nope." She was warm and comfy, right where she was.

"Good." There was a smile in his voice. He reached down, grabbed one of the robes and covered them.

She closed her eyes. The wind was roaring away and it sounded like it was sleeting again, but she was smiling. They couldn't stay like this forever, but she wasn't opposed to spending a few more days this way.

"It's sleeting. The roads will be covered in ice— impassable." He looked up at her. "Damn the bad luck." And then he was grinning from ear to ear.

At some point, Cassie drifted off to sleep. He'd shifted them so she wasn't smooshed beneath him, but she ended up cradled along his side with her cheek against his chest. Where she fit. He ran his hand along the curve of her back and dropped a kiss on top of her head. It kept him awake—which meant he wouldn't wake up and find that their night had been a dream. He'd dreamed of her for years. None of his dreams had come close to the reality. He couldn't remember the last time he'd felt so happy. But he did.

This had really happened. He'd made love to Cassie—several times. With any luck, that would be on today's agenda, too. But if he didn't get up and add some wood to the fire, they'd go from cuddled up and comfy to teeth-chattering and blue.

He moved slowly. Inch by inch, he eased out from under her. Since he'd covered them in their robes, he wrapped himself in a throw and tiptoed across the thick braided rug to the fireplace.

He smiled at the sight of Bert and Ernie surrounding the puppies. From overhead, they resembled a circular patchwork rug. The dogs gave him a couple of eager tail thumps before burrowing back in and dozing off.

It wasn't easy to quietly add logs to a fire. He tried—and failed.

"That's quite a view," she murmured.

He looked over his shoulder and paused. "Mine's better." Damn, she was beautiful. Mussed hair, sleepy eyes, propped on her side with bare shoulders and a soft smile. He took a minute to memorize everything about this—everything about her.

"I don't know." She bobbed her eyebrows.

He glanced down. The throw covered his shoulders and hung to the top of his thighs but his long legs and feet were bare. "I was planning on coming back to you pretty quick."

"Oh good." She smiled and lay back, tugging the covers up.

By the time he had the fire stoked high and warm, the dogs had other ideas. Bert and Ernie stretched and headed straight for the door while the puppies began their hunger song.

"Or not." Cassie sat up. "Here." She handed him his robe. "Duty calls."

He pulled on the robe, stepped into his boots, and gave the dogs a quick pat before he opened the door. It was biting cold and misting, leaving almost no visibility. "Let's make this fast." He pulled the door shut behind him and stared out into the gray. Hell, even the weather couldn't dim his good mood.

Until a faint spot of light started heading their way. Closer and closer until he realized it was a snowcat.

Bert and Ernie started barking and headed back to the porch.

"Y'all okay?" An older man, bundled in ski gear, climbed off the vehicle. "Name's Marvin Green. I own this little cabin." He held out his hand.

"Good to meet you." Sterling shook the man's hand. "We're doing fine." He patted Bert and Ernie. "I'm thankful you went with a gas water heater and stove."

"I'm from up north." He chuckled. "It never occurred to me to go any other way."

Sterling wasn't exactly dressed for company, neither was Cassie, but it'd be rude to leave their host out in the snow. "I was about to make a pot of coffee, if you want to come in?"

"I won't say no to coffee." The man stomped the snow off his boots.

"Let me give Cassie a heads-up."

"I thought you were alone out here." He didn't sound unhappy, just surprised.

"I was supposed to be. It's too long a story to tell out in this cold."

Marvin chuckled again. "Fair enough."

Sterling opened the door to find Cassie enveloped in the too-big snowflake robe, sitting before the fire with the puppies. "We have company."

Cassie's eyes went round.

Sterling winked at her, then stepped aside so the dogs and Mr. Green could come inside. "Marvin Green this is Cassie Lafferty. Cassie, this is Mr. Green."

"Marvin suits me just fine. I apologize for dropping in, but I wanted to see how you're faring out here." He took off his ski coat and hung it on the peg next to Sterling's, giving Sterling the chance to inspect the man.

Marvin Green was tall and fit, his white hair thick and trimmed. He had intelligent eyes and was smiling the moment he set eyes on the puppies. "You two look like you've got your hands full."

Sterling swallowed back a yawn. "That's for sure."

"How'd you get these little fellas?" Marvin came around the couch to get a closer look at the puppies. "They're tiny little things, aren't they?"

"They are." Cassie nodded, her gaze shifting from the puppy she was feeding to Marvin Green. "I work at the vet clinic. These two were dropped off before I headed home, and with the storm coming, I knew they'd be better off coming with me."

"I'd say so." Marvin nodded.

Sterling turned on the coffee, filled Bert and Ernie's bowls, and headed into the living room. He picked up the bigger pup, howling like his life was over, and the second bottle. "Have a seat, Mr. Green. The coffee will be ready soon."

"Marvin, please." The man in the recliner. "Don't mind if I do. I already stopped at the other two cabins. They're both unoccupied, so it was more about checking pipes than anything else."

"How is it possible we've never met before? I've lived here my whole life and know just about every face hereabouts." She set aside the empty bottle and cleaned up the puppy.

"I tend to keep to myself, I suppose. I bought the place and had everything built before I came down. I guess I've been here about six months now. Moved to get away from the cold and snow." He laughed. "Guess it followed me."

"It's a nice change for us." Cassie laughed, too. "Welcome to Texas. Every day is a new season."

Cassie's laugh. Her smile. Sterling took it all in.

"The news said it'll stick around for another day or two, then it'll all melt." Marvin sat back.

Cassie glanced at Sterling, her smile wavering.

He did his damndest to smile. He'd take whatever time they had, but he was hoping the weatherman was off on his prediction. By a day or two—or a week.

Cassie stood, the pup wriggling and squirming in her arms. "I'll get the coffee if you don't mind holding this one, Marvin?"

The older man lit up. "I do not mind. Been a while since I had a dog around. I think it's high time I started looking for one." He took the puppy and rested it against his chest. "Tiny fella."

"I can help you out with that." Cassie headed into the kitchen. "My brother, Buzz Lafferty, is the vet in town, and we're always getting strays or drop-offs that need a forever family."

"I'd appreciate you keeping an eye out for me. Not one quite so young." He covered the puppy with his hand. "My wife and I always had a dog. She'd say a family was only complete once you had a dog. We had dogs instead of kids."

"Is she here with you?" Cassie glanced up from the kitchen. "How do you like your coffee, Marvin? Not that we have anything to doctor it."

Marvin chuckled. "Black, please." He patted the puppy again. "My Katherine's been gone on four years now." And the man was grieving.

"I'm sorry for your loss." Sterling meant it. He'd been out of his mind after losing Cassie—and she was alive and well. To know that she was no longer in the world, living and breathing and happy? It was a pain he didn't want to imagine.

"I am, too. But we had thirty-seven good years together, so I'd say I'm a lucky man." His smile was wistful. "She was quite a woman. They don't make many women like her, that's for sure."

"What a gift to have one another for so long."

Cassie took a long look at the older man. "I'm sure you miss her."

Marvin glanced between Sterling and Cassie then. "You two strike me as being in the honeymoon phase still." He chuckled.

"Oh… No." Cassie stopped midway across the room, almost spilling the two cups of coffee she carried. "I was stranded on the side of the road and Sterling saw the emergency triangle I'd set up when he was driving by." She stared down at her robe. "I'm so grateful for the robe. It's all I have to wear until my clothes dry."

"Oh, well then. You okay?" Marvin's forehead creased heavily as he frowned. He turned to assess Sterling more thoroughly. "I can get you to town if you need. It'll take a while on the snow cat but I'm willing." The old man was looking out for her.

Sterling appreciated the man's concern but… He hoped like hell Cassie wouldn't choose to go with the old man. There was no way to ask her to stay, not without revealing more to Marvin Green than he wanted.

"I appreciate the offer." Cassie handed him a mug, her big blue eyes searching his. One brow cocked in question and he gave her a firm headshake, mouthing "Stay." Her answering smile instantly eased him. "I'm fine staying put. But thank you."

Now Marvin was reassessing the both of them. Sterling saw the older man's smile as he lifted his coffee cup to his mouth. "If you're sure?"

"I'm sure." Cassie returned to her spot on the floor. "Sterling and I aren't strangers." Her confession surprised him. "We've known each other for years. Not that this was a planned reunion—"

"That's a nice way of putting it." Sterling sipped his coffee. "Took ten years off my life opening that car door and finding you that way." Sterling still didn't like thinking of how it could have turned out. "Her car skidded off the road and slammed into a fence." His gaze sought her out.

"That's how I met my wife—saving her. Nothing as serious as your story, mind you. I was visiting a cousin and went to a festival. Fourth of July, I think." Marvin Green paused, thinking. "It was hot." He shrugged. "Anyway, there was this beautiful girl. And when I say beautiful, I mean beautiful. One look and I knew she was it for me. To this day, that's the one thing I knew and never doubted." He smiled at Cassie, who smiled back.

That smile. He knew what Marvin Green was talking about. He remembered the first time he laid eyes on Cassie Lafferty—every detail.

"She was surrounded by fellas all vying for her hand but she wasn't impressed. If anything, she seemed to be looking for a way out. When she saw me, she paused just long enough for me to throw myself into the lake." He chuckled. "I yelled for help and guess who dived in to save me?" He shook his head, his gaze glossing over as he stared into the past. "I could swim, of course, but she didn't know that. She pulled me up onto the sand and knelt beside me to make sure I was all right, her dress soaked through and her hair dripping wet. I told her she could thank me for rescuing her from all that unwanted attention on our first date. All she could do was laugh."

Cassie was hugging her knees, totally engrossed in his story. "I'm guessing you had that first date?"

"That very night." He nodded. "We didn't go a day without seeing each other after that. Or laughing. Laughter was a big part of our life." He took a sip of his coffee. "A few weeks later, we were married." He finished off his coffee and stood. "I best get going before the rain starts up again. It was nice to meet the two of you."

Cassie was up, taking the puppy and shaking the man's hand. "When this is all over, I expect to see you in town. Come to the Christmas parade at least. It's a good place to meet folk."

"We'll see." He smiled. "You take care of these little ones."

"I will. And I'll keep an eye out for a companion for you. Or two." She carried the puppy back to the mat, waving Bert and Ernie over.

Sterling watched, then walked the older man to the door. "Good to meet you."

Marvin nodded. "You as well." He shrugged into his coat. "I was a detective, you know."

Sterling waited, sensing the older man had something important to tell him.

"I pick up on things." He glanced at Sterling's bag full of clothes, then eyed the Santa robe. "Might be this reunion was meant to be. It's none of my business, of course, but let me offer you a piece of advice." He paused until Sterling nodded. "Don't wait for the right time, make the time right. That way you won't miss out on life, son, or regret any wasted opportunities." He leaned forward to whisper. "If I were you and sweet on Miss Lafferty the way I think you are, then I'd call this time snowed in together an opportunity."

Sterling nodded. It was. And he wasn't going to waste it.

Chapter Ten

Cassie had managed to wait until Marvin Green left before she took a running leap at Sterling. Lucky for her, he caught her. The surprise on his face gave way to want the minute her lips touched his.

It was a long and lazy day. When they weren't wrapped up in each other, they took care of the puppies and made a healthy dent in their gift basket stash. It was late afternoon when the cabin was flooded with light.

"Is that the sun?" She pushed off his chest and sat up. *No no no*. They were supposed to have more time. Without the ice and snow, there was no reason to stay and nothing to stop Buzz from coming to get her.

"No." He tugged at her hand, attempting to pull her back against his chest. "Probably an alien spaceship with a big spotlight."

She stared down at him in disbelief. "That was my second guess."

He sat up and frowned. "Huh." He stood, not

in the least bit modest as he walked, completely naked, to look out the window. "No spaceships."

"Really? That's a surprise." She rested her chin on the back of the couch, contentedly ogling his sculpted ass and thighs. His scar. "Sterling?"

"Hmm?" He turned.

Now that he was facing her, she was having a hard time forming words. They might have spent the day exploring each other, but she was just as flustered over the sight of his body as ever.

"You're blushing." He smiled, heading back to the couch.

"You're seeing things." She tilted her head for a kiss. "Can I ask you something?"

He kissed her and sat, pulling a throw over them. "Fire away."

"What happened to you? Your scar?" She peered up at him. "Was it a rodeo accident? Another drunken car trip? What?"

He smiled as he stared into the fire. "That's all on me. I was stupid. Looking back, I did a whole hell of a lot of stupid things." He ran a hand over his face. "I'd had my best ride and stuck the landing, but I was too busy scanning the crowd to know the bull was on me. Broke my back. Punctured a lung."

Cassie slid her arms around his waist and burrowed closer. He'd wanted to be the best bull rider. *Wanted* wasn't the right word. *Compelled* was more like it. His father had made it into an obsession for Sterling. "Who were you looking for?" She suspected she knew the answer.

"My father."

Her hold tightened, but she stayed silent. She wasn't one to hate, it went against her nature. Billy Ford was the exception. He was a brutal man—with words and his hands. Poor Sterling had to bear the brunt of the man's abuse for years. When Sterling moved to Granite Falls, all that had changed. His father was in jail and Sterling was free to start again. Here, with her, she'd thought he was happy. He'd showered her with all the love he'd likely stored away for years.

"After I left... Well, I was a mess. I didn't know what way was up. I was the one drinking and passing out. My father was the one dragging me along and kept me going. He said he was training me, but mostly, I was his free ride. If I was drunk, I didn't care if he was taking my money or driving around in my truck. Before too long, we were both drinking hard and picking fights—fights I'd have to finish." Sterling's laugh was bitter. "He never wanted to see me succeed, he wanted money. The night of my accident, we fought. He cut me down, telling me what a disappointment I was and how ashamed he was of me. I pushed back, calling him a piss-poor father and a mean drunk. A few punches were thrown."

She turned her face into his side.

"It wasn't like it hadn't happened before. But I'd taken a hard knock to the head. My whole ride, it was like I was in slow motion. I made it through, somehow. Until the bull did a tap dance on my spine, that is."

"I'm so, so sorry."

"I'm okay now, Cassie." He pressed a kiss to the top of her head. "It wasn't all bad. The urge to impress my father or win his approval vanished that day. He watched them put me in the ambulance, but he disappeared into the crowd instead of coming with me to the hospital."

Her heart ached for him. He'd suffered mentally and physically. Alone.

"I was too stubborn and prideful for too long. There's nothing like being left in a hospital for weeks and learning to walk again to humble a man." He held her away from him then. "I shouldn't have believed a word he said to me."

"He's your father." It was a whisper. They were entering dangerous territory here. She wasn't sure she was prepared to talk about what had happened between them.

"He was never my father. He was a sperm donor." He pulled her back into his arms.

The comment clanged about in her head. "Sterling." She pulled free of his hold. "I can't believe we're so stupid." She tugged the robe tight and tied the waist. "Careless." Her lungs were desperate for air.

"What?" He stood, reaching for her.

"We didn't use any protection, Sterling." She shook her head, her voice rising higher and higher until Bert and Ernie ran to her side to check on her.

Sterling froze.

"What are we going to do?" It's not like there was much they could do.

His hands gripped her shoulders. "It'll be okay."

She shrugged off his touch. "You can't say that. You don't know that." She sank onto the couch, dread flooding her every cell. "Let's have sex. Sure, why not." Her voice was shaking. "Why think it through—think about the possible consequences—when we're cocooned up here without a care in the world right now?"

He crouched in front of her. "I wasn't thinking straight. I'm sorry."

"Neither one of us were." But she couldn't look at him. "If I'd kept my mouth closed, none of this would have happened."

"And that would be a damn shame."

She stared at him. "Are you serious? We agreed this was a no-strings, no-expectations sort of scenario—"

"That was before you might be pregnant."

She couldn't believe what he was saying. "Stop." She swallowed hard. "You have a life you want to get back to. A life that doesn't include me. I do, too. What are you implying? That you're ready to forget all that and settle? That we change everything because of one careless mistake?" The look on his face was unnerving. Whatever he was considering, the hair along the back of her neck pricked up. "No." She shook her head. "Don't you dare say something stupid because of this. You didn't love me five minutes ago, don't you dare say it now. I'd have no choice but to hate you, then."

His lips were pressed into a tight line.

"I'm going to take a shower." She brushed past him and into the bathroom, closing the door behind her. It was so cold she could see her breath, but it barely registered. How had this happened? She knew how it had happened, she'd enjoyed each and every time to the fullest extent. How could her body ache for him and her heart be so close to coming apart? How had she let this happen? She clicked on the heater and turned on the shower faucets.

It'll be okay. In what world would having a… baby with Sterling be okay? She had a hard time thinking the word *baby*. She wasn't ready to have one. No matter how sincere he'd looked or how confident he'd sounded, it didn't ring true.

She shrugged out of the robe and stepped beneath the warm water.

She poured a healthy dollop of peppermint onto the loofah and started scrubbing, but her brain kept on turning. Her heart softened at the memory of how gentle he'd been with the puppies. She shook her head and continued scrubbing. He'd taken care of her, too. Asked her to stay. Wrapped her up and held her through the night. It didn't matter that he'd listened to her without judgment or agenda. It didn't matter that the last twenty-four hours were quite possibly the best in her existence. She'd lied to herself all this time and now she'd suffer for it. She loved Sterling. Her heart had never truly given him up. She loved him and wanted him to be happy. Baby or not, she wouldn't let him settle for her.

What the hell was he supposed to do now? If he told her how he felt about her, she wouldn't believe him. She'd hate him. He ran both hands through his hair and paced the length of the open-concept kitchen and living room. If she was going to listen to him, he'd have to leave his emotions out of it. He shook his head and braced both hands against the living room's windowsill.

The little sunshine they'd had hadn't done much good on the ice and snow. It was likely temps would drop below freezing again tonight. He didn't mind. He was in no hurry to say goodbye. Not now. It was going to be hard but they had to talk through this.

"Is it snowing?" Her voice had him spinning on his heel.

He shook his head, noting how red-faced and puffy-eyed she looked. "You want to borrow some clothes?" He held up a pair of drawstring gym pants and a T-shirt. "Although, the robe is probably warmer and more comfortable."

"I'm good." She joined him at the window. "Do you think things will clear up tomorrow?"

"It's Texas, it's hard to predict." If he had it his way, another norther would blow in. "Hungry?"

She shook her head.

"How about some music?" He pulled his battery-powered radio from his bag. "I found some more batteries and an all–Christmas carol station." He turned the knob and the strains of "The First Noel" filled the small cabin. "It's just about the only station that's not all static."

She smiled. "That's nice."

"You can sing along." He headed into the kitchen to scavenge for food. "I know you love Christmas carols. Especially 'Here Comes Santa Claus.'" He placed a couple of sausage rolls on a plate and pulled one of the macaroni boxes from the freezer. The box was still frozen. *Because it's been so damn cold.* He followed the directions on the box and put the mac in to bake. "Nothing fancy for dinner. But it'll be warm."

"Warm is good." She was humming.

He smiled, making them a cup of hot chocolate and adding extra marshmallows to hers. "Here." He handed her a mug.

"With extra marshmallows." Her puffy eyes met his. "That's sweet of you."

"I figure we could both use a drink." He sipped his hot chocolate, swallowed and followed it up with a big sigh. "That hits the spot."

She laughed. "I could go for something stiffer... But I guess I shouldn't." She took another sip. "This will do."

"Can we talk about this?" He braced himself for an immediate no.

"It's a little late to be acting responsible but... Better late than never, I guess?" She carried her mug to the kitchen bar and sat, looking defeated.

He caught her hand in his. "If we're having a baby, I want to be a part of its life." He hurried on before she could interrupt or argue with him. "We're in this together." He gave her hand a squeeze and let it go.

She turned her mug slowly, chewing on the inside of her lip. "Not *together* as in an obligatory marriage?"

From her tone, he could tell she didn't like the idea. "I mean *together* in whatever way suits us both best."

She stopped spinning her mug to glance up at him. "That's very diplomatic of you."

"Is it? I was aiming more for supportive." He shrugged. "Guess I need to work on that."

Her smile was slight and then it was gone. "We're in this together and we're in a wait-and-see situation?" She sipped her hot chocolate. "We can hammer out the specifics once we know if I…"

"Okay." Since he'd taken on the job, he'd become a planner. The not-knowing part was going to make planning a challenge. "Next topic."

"There's more?" She set her mug down, her eyes meeting his.

"We're still here." He pointed around the cabin. "There's still snow and ice outside." He glanced at the window. "We need protection."

Her blink was owlish. "Are you asking me if we're having more sex?" Her brows shot up on the last word.

"Am I?" He put a bowl of nuts on the counter and smiled her way. "I guess I should check the bathroom cabinets, just in case. Mr. Green seems to have thought of everything else."

Her mouth opened and closed.

"What are the chances, do you think?" He

couldn't take the distance. He came around the counter, moved in as close as he could and cradled her face in his hands. "I'm trying to make you laugh." He kissed her startled lips, running his fingers through her damp hair. "I did make you a guarantee."

Her breath was unsteady. "You did."

"You're surprised?" He pressed a kiss against each eye.

"I suppose I thought this whole…scare might change things." She stared up at him.

"Like me wanting you?" He frowned and shook his head. "I meant it when I said I'd always want you. Baby or not, that won't change."

"Sterling, I—"

His phone started ringing. "Hold that thought." He reached for his phone. "It's for you." He handed it over and went back into the kitchen.

"Hi, Buzz. I'm fine." She sipped her hot chocolate. "He's been making me rest… Yes. He even made me hot chocolate. Extra marshmallows…" She sighed. "Do you want me to hang up on you?" Then she froze, her eyes locking with his. "Tomorrow morning?… No, no, no. I'll ask him to drop me off… No, Buzz, I mean it." Another sigh. "Yep… Great. See you then… I love you, too." She put the phone on the bar. "The roads are being salted in the early morning. It should be clear to get back into town."

"Okay. Well, that sucks." He stared blindly at the mess he'd made on the counter. "I'm going to miss the late-night puppy feedings."

Her surprised laughter took the edge off the bad news.

They ate their macaroni and sausage rolls in silence. Bert and Ernie left the puppies to sit at their feet, hoping for a dropped noodle or piece of sausage. The puppies must have noticed the absence of their nest-warmers, because the howling started.

Sterling grinned and set his mostly clean plate on the floor. "I'll get their dinner ready."

After the pups were fed and Bert and Ernie went out and ate their kibble, he turned up the music and waited for Cassie to pick a puzzle.

"This one." She held up the Christmas tree puzzle.

"One thousand pieces of a decorated Christmas tree. That won't take long." He sat by the coffee table and started sorting out the border pieces—the way she preferred it. He glanced her way to find her smiling at him. "Am I doing it right this time?"

"Sterling…" She shook her head and crawled the few feet to reach him. But she didn't stop there. She climbed onto his lap. Her warm breath fanned across his face. Her legs straddled him, her robe parting as she bent to kiss him.

"I thought—" he broke off as her tongue swept along the seam of his mouth "—we were—" he groaned when she nipped at his lower lip "—doing a…" She sucked his lower-lip into his mouth. "Oh, to hell with it." His hands slid up her thighs to grip her hips.

She gasped when he pulled aside her robe and sucked the peak of one breast into his mouth.

Feeling the skin go taut and puckered made him ache. Knowing he brought her pleasure was both empowering and humbling.

Her fingers twined into his thick hair as she arched into him. She moaned when he sucked her deep and used his tongue to drive her wild.

He wasn't going to waste a minute of the time remaining. He hadn't discovered a secret condom stash in the cabin, so he'd have to improvise. As much as he wanted to be buried inside of her, he resisted. The rest of the night was spent making sure he kissed and tasted and loved every inch of her. When she rested her head on his chest and her body relaxed in sleep, he held her close. *I love you.*

He didn't sleep. He couldn't. When the sun was streaming in and the birds were making all sorts of a ruckus outside, he could delay things no longer. He nuzzled his nose along her throat. "The sun's up. We'd best get a move on or Buzz'll be pounding on the door in no time."

She shook her head and stayed as she was.

He pressed a kiss to her forehead and held her tighter. "I was hoping for sleet or ice or snow while we slept."

She rolled over so her chin rested on his chest. "That would have been nice." She seemed to be looking for something.

He smoothed her hair back. "What are you thinking? Let it out."

"You might regret that." She stared up into his eyes. "When you came back to Granite Falls before and ran into Buzz what, exactly, happened?"

Which wasn't what he expected. He'd rather leave that alone—he didn't want to be responsible for putting any wedge between her and her brother. "We fought."

"You mean, he fought and you didn't fight back?" She frowned at him. "Everyone has been lying to me. They call it *protecting* me, but... I'm not in the mood to deal with him hovering and asking a ton of questions. I'm afraid I'll wind up chewing him out in front of the kids." She ran a finger down the middle of his chest. "Maybe it'd be best if I went home."

He propped himself on his side. "I understand why you're mad and you should talk to him. Right now, he's worried about you—more than usual.

The car accident was bad enough. But you've been trapped with me for three whole nights."

She caught his hand in hers. "Why are you taking his side? After everything he's said and done?"

"I'm not taking his side. Tell him how you feel—don't back down. I think he'll listen." He hoped so. Buzz and Cassie had their disagreements, but they were unwaveringly loyal. If Cassie pushed on this, Buzz would back off. "But I can't fault him for loving and worrying about you. You know my family—where I come from. I've never had someone looking out for me the way he watches over you. Overprotective or not, it's cool."

She shook her head, but she was smiling. "How about I tell him you want to trade places with me for a week or two? That might be enough time to get you to change your mind."

He chuckled. "Maybe. But, with Buzz, I always know where I stand." He twined one of her long curls around his finger. "When my dad was around, I never knew who I'd be dealing with from one day to the next. Would he be quiet and sullen or angry and aggressive? Would he dish out praise or pour on the criticism? No matter what his mood was, I never measured up. And if my own father felt that way, how could anyone else feel otherwise?" Why the hell had he said any of that? He tugged at the curl, trying to lighten the mood. "Basically, my frame of reference for healthy family interactions is screwed up, so I probably have nothing useful to say here." His chuckle was forced.

She sniffed, her eyes full of tears. "All right, I'll go easy on Buzz. Sort of."

He nodded but didn't add anything else. He'd done the counseling sessions his AA leader had recommended, but he knew he was a work in progress. He'd had years of his father bearing down on him and picking him apart. He couldn't just turn all that off with the snap of his fingers, no matter how much he wished that were the case.

"I'm sorry your father wasn't there for you. I can't imagine how hard that must be." She brushed her fingertips along his jaw. "You know that what he said and did wasn't your fault, right? That he was the problem, not you. It's hard to see that when you're in an abusive relationship." There was such tenderness in her eyes, he leaned closer to her to soak it in. "If you hear a thing often enough, you start to believe it."

The truth of those words rolled over him. She had her own experience with an abusive person— she understood better than most. Sterling's anger was tempered with bitterness then. "When my father showed up here, I wanted to go along with this new, reformed version and rewrite who he was. I wanted him to be someone else, someone I could rely on—like what you and Buzz and your folks have. I'd seen what family could be and I wanted it." He'd ached for it. "He was good. Right from the get-go, he teased me about you. Then he stepped it up, more sympathetic and telling me I was kidding myself and that I was no good for you. Then he went deep, saying you'd wind up like my mom, sad and resentful—and gone." He stared into the fire. "The liquor progressed, too. Starting with a friendly beer, moving to whiskey. In the end, he was filling up shot glasses until I threw up or passed out."

She just stared at him now, her mouth parted.

"I made all these realizations while I lay staring up at the hospital ceiling. He'd played me. He'd taken what mattered most to me, used me, then left me to fend for myself. But he wasn't wrong about not deserving you. What sort of man can be talked into questioning something he knows is true?" He frowned, squeezing her hands. "I was an ass and I own that. I said mean things to push you away, and those words will haunt me for the rest of my life." He shook his head. "As soon as I was on my feet and sobered up, I came to find you. I had to apologize."

"But Buzz stopped you."

"I didn't blame him. I still don't. He said you

were happy and had moved on and I didn't want to get in the way of that." He ran his fingers through his hair. "You being happy made it easier to walk away."

Her face was blank and pale, but her eyes remained locked with his.

He'd said it. He'd gotten all the words out.

"I was in the beginning," she whispered. "But, slowly, I became afraid. It took a while to tell Buzz the truth. I was scared. And when I did, Buzz lost it. Well, you know." Her gaze swept over his nose. "I'm thinking your visit must have been right around the time I… ended things." She blew out a slow breath. "Buzz was all rage back then. But he had no right to lash out at you. Or to keep you away."

Sterling would've been the same. He'd hurt Cassie once. After what she'd been through, it made sense Buzz wasn't up for giving him a second chance. It wasn't much, but it fit with the little Buzz had let slip out. "Who was he? Where is he?" His jaw was clenched so tight it hurt.

"Gone." She waved her hand dismissively. "Not worth a thought. I'd rather not mention him again."

Message received. Besides, he was all too happy to stay as they were. Close, holding hands, being together. He could stare into her blue eyes for hours and still want more.

"I'll get dressed." She stood. "Can I borrow those clothes?"

He itched to reach out for her. "Help yourself."

She carried the clothes into the bedroom and closed the door behind her. *Well, hell.* He loved her. He loved her too much to let her go without putting up a fight. Baby or not, he wanted them to have a second chance. This time, he'd make sure she knew how much she meant to him every damn day.

Chapter Eleven

Her eyes hurt. Her lungs ached. The pain in her chest was sharp and unrelenting. His words were on repeat, cycling through her brain over and over. Whatever anger or hurt she'd carried with her was gone. That he'd been used as a doormat by the one person who should have given him unconditional love sliced her heart in two. His own father had made him feel unworthy of love. Worse, he'd spent most of the last six years broken, recovering and alone. She was glad he'd shared everything with her. His apology hadn't just ticked her name off his list, it had explained everything. It didn't make it better, but there were no more unanswered questions.

Except how to accept this was over. That their short-lived affair was just that—versus the beginning of their second chance.

He hadn't been looking for a second chance when he came here. He was working through his apologies list, that was all. This was part of his recovery process, a way to separate the human person from the bad disease and let go of the shame of his addiction. She wanted Sterling to see that he was human, a good human, and neither his father or his addiction defined him.

As long as she managed to make it inside Buzz and Jenna's house without bursting into tears, she'd be fine. Between the kids and the dogs, there'd be plenty to distract her from the knife slicing through her heart.

Sterling was staring straight ahead. If he hadn't been white-knuckling the steering wheel or clenching his jaw, she'd have thought he was fine with what was happening. It was a relief to know he wasn't.

They reached the city limits and her words erupted. "I'll let you know. I'll… Will you be here?"

"I'm going to stay through the holidays." He nodded. "Parades and stuff. You know. I haven't done any of that in a while."

"And you have a pirate Santa to keep you in the holiday spirit." Her laugh was forced.

He was silent as they rolled up in front of Buzz's house. "I'm here. If you need anything. To talk or whatever… I'm here."

She hugged the puppy box to her chest. "Then, why does it feel like we're saying goodbye?"

"We're not saying goodbye." He was adamant.

He stared at her a few more seconds, then climbed down from the truck.

Cassie watched as the front door opened and three of the four kids came running out. "All right, boys, let's go." Sterling opened her door and took the puppy box while she, Bert and Ernie got out. No sooner had her feet touched the ground than Frannie had her arms wrapped about her thighs.

"Cassie, Cassie. You awe hewa."

She reached down to hug her niece back. "I am here. And my friend, Sterling, has something I need your help with."

Frannie took her hand and led Cassie to Sterling. "Hello. Momma says to be nice to you. Buzz says you awe a pain in his—"

"Buzz said not to repeat that, Frannie." Garrett, her only nephew, regarded his little sister with exasperation. "I'm Garrett. This is Frannie. And that's Monica." He pointed at his big sister who was slowly navigating the icy walk. "My little sister, Biddy, is inside. She's not too steady at walking yet. She'd probably fall over in the snow and start crying." He frowned.

"Did Buzz send you outside to stop him from coming in?" Cassie asked, shielding her eyes from the sun's reflection off the snow.

Monica, Garrett and Frannie all shrugged.

"Come on, Sterling." Cassie shook her head,

patting her thigh for the dogs. "Come on, boys, you can go play with Shaggy, Roscoe and Scooter."

"We have a lot of dogs," Garrett told Sterling. "Do you have a dog?"

"I'm a fan, but I don't have one."

"I'm sorry." Garrett held open the front door and called out, "They're here."

"That was loud, Gawwett." Frannie covered her ears. "Can we see what's in the box now?" She clapped her hands.

"Welcome home." Jenna came out of the kitchen. "Come in, come in." She steered the group into the front parlor before taking in Cassie's clothes. "What are you wearing?"

"I had to borrow clothes. I'm not sure mine will recover—even with a good washing." Cassie hugged her almost sister-in-law.

"Are you all right?" Jenna whispered for her ears only.

"I don't know." She struggled to hold back tears.

Jenna patted her back. "Sterling." She held out her hand. "We finally meet. I'm Jenna, Cassie's sister-in-law. Almost."

"That's how you're going to introduce yourself?" Buzz leaned against the doorframe leading into the parlor. "You're also my soon-to-be wife."

"Yes, well, I didn't know if you were going to make an appearance or not." Jenna shot him a look.

Cassie loved that Jenna had no problem going toe-to-toe with her brother. How she manages to juggle her four younger half siblings, three dogs and Buzz was a mystery. As far as Cassie was concerned, Jenna was near saintly.

"Sterling." Buzz nodded.

"Buzz." He nodded in return.

"It's so nice that this won't be the least bit awkward." She glared at her brother. "No need to jump right into 'thank-yous' or anything." She crossed her arms over her chest. "You, my darling brother, have some explaining to do."

"Should the kids go upstairs?" Jenna asked.

"To who? You?" Buzz pushed off the wall. "Sterling and I don't need to explain anything to each other."

"So, that's a yes?" Jenna asked.

"Then, explain it to me." Cassie pushed back "You think what you did to Sterling was protecting me?"

"Dammit, Cassie, you don't understand." Buzz glanced Sterling's way.

"Okay, kids, let's go upstairs and watch a Christmas movie." Jenna sort of herded the three kids from the room. "You pick one out and I'll be up in a minute."

"I've got this, Jenna. Just make sure to tell me all the details after." Monica was all teenager, she loved to stay up-to-date on all the juicy gossip.

"Okay." Jenna waved, then came back into the parlor. "Buzz, if Frannie walks around chanting *dammit* like she did when you said *shit*, I'll wash both of your mouths out with soap."

Cassie almost laughed at the imagery. Almost. She bet Jenna would do it, too.

Buzz ran a hand along the back of his neck, breathing deeply.

"We could all sit down and attempt to have a *calm*, adult conversation?" Jenna suggested.

"That's not necessary." Sterling set the puppy box on the table and turned to Buzz. "I'm just dropping Cassie off. I get it. She's your sister and you want what's best for her."

"He gets it." Buzz pointed at Sterling.

"I don't. How the hell can you justify breaking his nose, pummeling him senseless and chasing him out of town?" Cassie stared back and forth between the two of them.

"For the record, I never said you pummeled me senseless." Sterling crossed his arms over his chest.

"And no one chased him out of town. Angus and Dougal just escorted him to the city limits." Buzz's voice faded out and he cleared his throat.

"They did *what*?" Cassie was horrified. No wonder Sterling was on the fence about doing business with the McCarricks. She was surprised he hadn't passed on working with them from the get-go.

"I could have handled it better." Buzz had the decency to look remorseful. "But he hurt you so bad—"

"That doesn't give you the right to raise a hand against him." Cassie cut him off. "It's never okay to get physical, Buzz. You know that." She didn't think as she rested her hand on Sterling's arm. "We've made our peace. He took care of me. He fed me and clothed me and woke up every two hours to help me with the puppies."

"Puppies?" Jenna's went round. "More puppies?"

"They'll go with me, don't worry." Cassie gave her a reassuring smile. "I need you to listen to me, Buzz, please. This needs to stop. After all he's done for me and the dogs and the puppies, you no longer have any reason to dislike him. Stop being such a dick. What happened in the past is done. If I can forgive Sterling, you have no excuse not to do the same."

"You do?" Sterling's hand covered hers.

She blinked rapidly, willing the tears not to start. "Of course I do. Sterling…" She shook her head and blinked some more. The look of anguish on his face was too much. "I forgive you."

There was a thud and wailing from upstairs and both Jenna and Buzz looked alarmed.

"I'll go," Jenna offered.

"No. Stay." Buzz headed for the door.

"Aunt Cassie, Frannie wants you," Garrett yelled down. "She's being a big baby about it, too."

Buzz stopped, shooting Cassie a long-suffering look.

"Am not. I missed you, Aunt Cassie." Frannie called back. "You awe wude, Gawwett."

Cassie smiled.

"It doesn't sound like anyone's bleeding." Jenna relaxed.

Sterling's gaze fell from hers, and his jaw clenched tight, but he nodded. "Sounds like you're needed and I should get going."

Her hand tightened on his arm, but he didn't slow. She stood, her heart in knots, as he headed down the entry hall. When the front door closed, the knots tightened. She moved to the front window and watched as he walked through the snow and climbed into his vehicle. He started the ignition, but the truck didn't move. He sat in the there, his hands running through his hair and his head shaking.

Cassie gripped the back of the chair, willing him to look her way. Instead, he scrubbed his hands over his face, put the truck in gear, and pulled away and he was gone, taking her heart with him.

"Cassie?" Jenna's hand rested on her shoulder.

"I… I need to freshen up." She couldn't make eye contact or the dam would break.

"Use my bathroom. Soak in the tub." Jenna took her hand and led her to the stairs.

"Cassie?" Buzz called after her.

"I can't argue with you right now, Buzz. I'm… exhausted." She concentrated on putting one foot in front of the other and keeping her breathing steady. Jenna kept quiet, filling the bath and leaving her fresh clothes and toiletries.

"Do you need anything else?" Jenna asked, her hand on the doorknob. "Do you want to talk?"

Cassie shook her head, but the sobs started and Jenna wrapped her up in a fierce hug. "It's okay, Cassie. Whatever it is, it'll be okay. You just let it all out."

She couldn't stop if she wanted to. She'd learned the horrible truth behind all her heartache. Instead of making things better, it made them ten times worse. Especially now that he was gone. She wanted his arms around her. "Sterling," she whispered.

"I know, Cassie. I saw you." Jenna kept on rocking her. "Love isn't easy."

"I love him, but…how do I make him love me?" She held on to Jenna and cried herself out.

For days, Sterling felt adrift. Every time he started to reach out to Cassie, to tell her he loved her, her warning stopped him short. Would she really hate him? Or that he'd tell her he loved her out of obligation for their possible baby?

Their baby. That was a whole other issue. He'd said he'd be there for her and he'd meant it. But what the hell did he know about being a father? A good father? Because, dammit, he would be a good father.

When he wasn't thinking in circles, he checked in with Yvonne, caught up on email, made calls just like before. He met with the McCarricks and wound up helping clear out the Main Street Park. It felt good to do something—to help others. He went back two days in a row, but he never caught sight of Cassie. Then again, it might be bad for her to do anything too strenuous—if she was pregnant.

He thought about that a lot. A baby. Cassie. The family they could have and how good things could be. But if she was pregnant, how was he ever going to tell her he loved her and have her believe it? Which put him back at the beginning with no answer to the fundamental question. *What the hell am I supposed to do?*

When Marvin Green stopped by, he offered to chop down some of the dead trees around the cabin for firewood. Marvin happily took him up on his offer but wasn't happy to find Sterling still at it hours later.

"You working through something?" Marvin stood watching as Sterling swung the axe, over and over. "You've got that look."

"Look?" Sterling kept going.

"Far off. Setting things right in your mind. Making plans. Fixing problems. That sort of thing." Marvin sat on one of the stumps, out of harm's way.

"Chopping wood can do all that?" He paused to laugh. "Well, damn. I wish someone would've told me before I started drinking."

"That's what people say." Marvin slapped his thigh and hooted with laughter. "It never worked for me either."

He stopped chopping and took a long swig of water. "What did?"

"Talk through it, mostly." He shrugged. "Sometimes with Katherine. Other times, I talked to the damn dog. They listen pretty well, you know."

Bert and Ernie had been good listeners—especially if he snuck them a treat or two.

Marvin's gaze was laser focused. "In my experience, only two things can wear on a man like this." He pointed at the dozens of logs Sterling had chopped. "Love and money. Since you're willing to shell out the dough to stay in one of my overpriced cabins, I'm thinking it's not money. Plus, I have eyes, son. When did she leave?"

"I'm not paying, the company is." But he didn't dispute the rest.

"From where I was sitting, she wasn't giving you the stink eye." He scratched his chin. "Is there a particular reason you two aren't making Christmas cookies or canoodling under the mistletoe?"

He laughed. "Canoodling, huh?" He could add that to the list. Right by *nooky*.

"Don't knock it 'til you try it."

Sterling set down the axe and sat on a stump beside the older man. "I guess I could get some mistletoe."

Mr. Green looked at him. "Something tells me you won't."

"I'm not sure canoodling is enough to fix things." He took of his brown felt cowboy hat and ran his fingers through his hair. "I'm not…"

"You take your time putting the words together. I've got all the time in the world." He crossed his legs and settled in.

"I did something years back—"

"You were how old?"

"Nineteen." Old enough to know better. "I hurt her—the kind of hurt that leaves permanent marks on the inside."

Marvin nodded. "Hmm. You apologize?"

"Finally. Took longer than I'd like—"

"And what did she say?"

"She forgave me. She said she did, anyway." He stared up at the mottled gray sky overhead.

"Any reason not to believe her?"

"No." He shook his head. "It sounds easy enough but there's…more to it." He glanced at the older man.

"Something you don't want to share." He nodded. "I respect a man that doesn't kiss and tell." He reached over and clapped Sterling on the shoulder. "Seems to me you're holding yourself back. Take some time to figure out why that is. Once you know that, I have a feeling everything else will fall into place." He stood. "Now my old bones are aching and it'll be dark soon, so I'm heading home. You'd be wise to do the same. Take what you need and come back later."

Sterling stood. "'Night."

"You get some sleep." The older man patted his arm and headed back down the road Sterling had cleared with Marvin's tractor earlier.

He stuck his hat on his head and took his time walking back to his cabin. Without the round-the-clock feedings, Bert and Ernie trailing after him, or Cassie smiling at him from the couch, no amount of firewood could warm the place up.

Marvin Green was right. He was holding himself back. His father had always been angry. He'd lived rough, making bad choices that had landed him in jail more times than Sterling could count. His father had gone from an angry young man to a mean-and-angry old man. Breaking his back had severed the need for his father's approval, but it didn't quite erase the damage he'd done.

Like being good enough for Cassie. Even though he knew his father had done a number on him, he'd planted a seed of doubt Sterling couldn't silence. He went inside, hung his cowboy hat on one peg and his thick coat on the other. He eyed his phone for a good ten minutes before he picked it up and dialed the number of his father's retirement community.

He wasn't calling to make amends with the old man, he was calling to confirm what he already knew. He wasn't his father. He'd never be his father.

"Shady Oaks Retirement Home." He often wondered how the receptionist managed to stay so chipper when she had to deal with people like his father.

"Good evening. I was wondering if Billy Ford was still up and causing trouble."

"Well, hi there, Sterling. Of course, he is. As ornery as an old goat. He's been sneaking off and smoking, too." She sighed. "If he keeps that up, he'll wind up with pneumonia again. Maybe you can talk some sense into him. You make sure to stop by and tell me hello when you visit next."

"Will do."

"All right, I'll transfer you."

Sterling stood in the middle of the living room, his gaze settling on the two robes draped over the corner of the couch.

"Who is this?" his father grumbled. "I know it can't be my son. He must have died as it's been so long since I heard from him." He started coughing then.

"Dad." Sterling pinched the bridge of his nose. "How are they treating you?"

"You'd know if you ever visited." He mumbled something. "I get poked and prodded and flipped like a fish most days." More coughing. This bout lasted awhile.

His father refused to move around, and as a result, his skin was breaking down. "It's to help with the bed sores, Dad."

"I don't know what nonsense you're talking about."

"On your back—"

"When are you picking me up?" He wheezed, then cleared his throat. "How much longer do I have to stay here? Don't you know they feed me slop that ain't fit for hogs? They drag me outside to get sunshine even when I tell them no. A good son wouldn't leave his father here. It ain't right, I tell you." He carried on. It was the same every time he called. Sterling had learned it was better to tune him out versus trying to engage until his father was done. He ranted and coughed and ranted some more.

A little over three years ago, when he was just starting to get his life on track, he'd picked his father up from the county jail and brought him to his small house. His father ranted and railed and complained about everything. Every time Sterling went on the road, he'd worried what he'd come home to. Sometimes, his things were gone. Other times, there'd be new things his father had somehow managed to acquire. His health was declining, but he wouldn't take his meds or go to his doctor appointments. After his father had almost burned down his small house, Sterling knew it wasn't safe for his father to be alone. After learning one of his buddies was in the nursing home in Oklahoma, Sterling had taken him to visit. His father consented, signing all the papers and shooing him out the door. It started out fine. He had a friend and they raised hell—well, as much hell as you could raise in an assisted living facility. But it all had fallen apart when the two of them got into a fight and tried to capsize each other's wheelchairs. Since then, his father insisted that Sterling had dumped him against his will and made sure to remind him of that every time they spoke.

After another racking cough, his father asked, "Where are you?"

"I'm stuck in Texas—right in the middle of that snowstorm." Snow that was already melting away.

"Was it as bad as the news say? Or is it another one of them conspiracies?" His father was big into conspiracies. He loved a good tirade—even if there was no truth to what he was saying.

"It's pretty bad. Lost power pretty much all over. Took down some trees." He'd passed several utility trucks when he'd been in town last—it would take time to work through all the ranches and homesteads hereabouts.

"Where in Texas?" His father grumbled something under his breath. "My dinner's here. They're trying to poison me. I know you don't believe me, but you should try to eat this stuff." He took a deep, gasping breath.

"Granite Falls. Got a lead on some potential cutting horses." He didn't like the sound of his father's cough or how hard he was working to breathe.

"Granite Falls." He cackled. "I remember that pissant town. And that pretty little thing that dumped you. What was her name, Christy?"

He didn't answer. Somewhere along the line his father had rewritten things. He had broken them up, Cassie had dumped him. That way, his father washed his hands of the whole thing.

"She married with kids? Living in some fancy house having dinner parties? I bet she didn't even recognize you." He laughed again. "I bet she's fat and wears too much makeup." The last couple of words were more of a rasp.

"She's just the same as she always was." And he loved her just as much.

"You wouldn't admit it even if I was right." His father chuckled.

"I haven't mastered your talent for lying, Dad." He stopped himself. There was no point in arguing with his old man. "You on oxygen?"

"What did you say? It's a good thing you're not saying that to my face. All that time I spent teaching you to respect your elders and this is what I get? Too bad that bull didn't knock some sense into you instead of breaking your back." He was coughing so hard, it was a wonder he was able to breathe at all.

"You okay? You sound pretty rough." He paused. "You're not smoking. You know that'll make your COPD act up. Getting pneumonia again wouldn't be a good thing. Are you taking your medicine?"

"They shove it down my throat. When are you coming?"

"It depends. Last time I came, you threw everything within reach at me." He adjusted his hat on the peg. "The time before that, you spent thirty minutes ignoring me and another hour calling me a worthless son."

"You are." His father sniffed. "You should be ashamed."

"You're safe. You're fed. You're clean. You're getting medicine and physical therapy. Your nurse, Janice, calls me to give me updates all the time."

"That old cow." He grumbled, hacking away. "Whatever she's telling you, it's a lie."

The longer he listened to his father's labored breathing, the more concerned he got. "I'll try to come visit you in the next week." It wasn't too long a drive. If history repeated itself, the visit wouldn't last longer than an hour.

"Try?" He snapped. "What else do you have to do? Who else gives a rat's ass about you?" He went on, growing more agitated and coughing even harder. "It's me and you. Might as well make the best of it." He sighed. "It wouldn't hurt to remember all I've done for you. Warning you off that girl. Helping you get started rodeoing. Sending you off to your cousin for your high school years."

None of which was true. "I remember things differently." He regretted the words as soon as they were out. His father had every right to his own reality. It was listening to it all that was so exhausting.

"I bet you do. To hear you tell it, you lived a hard life. You don't have the foggiest idea what that means." His words were broken and thick. "You're too soft, boy—same as your worthless mother."

No phone call was complete without insulting his mother. "I'll talk to you soon—"

His father slammed the phone receiver down so hard Sterling's ear was ringing. It didn't matter, he'd heard what he needed to. His father was sick. He was a lying bastard who did his damndest to make Sterling feel lower than dirt, but he was still his father. Sick and old and frail and alone.

He didn't want to go see Billy Ford. He didn't want to have to sit and endure the insults and mood swings in person. But he'd never had the chance to say goodbye to his mother. If he'd known she was leaving, he'd have made sure nothing was left unsaid. Instead, he'd woken up to a house that no longer held any evidence she'd existed.

If he was truly going to make peace with his past, he owed it to himself to make sure that didn't happen with his father.

Chapter Twelve

Cassie hummed along with the Christmas music coming from the speakers of her brand-new car. Her old SUV had been totaled in the crash and insurance had paid for a new one. It was shiny and red and had just the right amount of get-up-and-go. After a long day at the clinic, she was finally headed home.

There were two weeks to Christmas, and there were planning meetings and float-decorating committees and caroling hayrides to chaperone. As much as she appreciated Jenna and Buzz including her in their family events, she was looking forward to the comfort of her own bed. Now that power had been restored, she wouldn't freeze, and at home, there'd be no nieces elbowing her in the hip or additional dogs crowding her to the very edge of the mattress. Tonight, it would just be the five of them. She, Bert, Ernie and the puppies. She'd been referring to the puppies as Big and Little to prevent too much confusion.

While the kids had offered up a constant stream

of name suggestions for the pups, none of them had been just right. Now that their eyes were open, and they were wrigglier than ever, the sooner she could start calling them by their names, the better.

She pulled up to the stop sign. If she went left, it was a straight shot to Sterling's cabin. If she turned right, she was minutes from home. Her foot stayed on the brake as she looked left, then right. Right. She should go home. That was the plan.

Why on earth would she turn left? She knew what she needed to say to Sterling next time she saw him. It wouldn't be easy, but it would put boundaries in place and, hopefully, her heart wouldn't be shattered when he left town.

"Right." She turned right, humming louder, then breaking into song.

Bert and Ernie sang along with her while the two pups squeaked and whimpered.

She was laughing, so she almost didn't see Sterling's truck in the oncoming lane. Almost. His eyes collided with hers in the few seconds it took for their vehicles to pass. That was all it took to make her heart skip a beat. In her rearview mirror, she saw his brake lights glow red. Anticipation slammed into her as the truck slowed.

"Is he stopping?" Sure enough, he pulled off onto the side of the road. That didn't mean... "He's not following us." Unfortunately, Bert and Ernie only continued to howl along to the music.

She went back to singing, her gaze bouncing between the road and the view behind her. No truck. No Sterling. Why was she so disappointed? "I need to calm down."

Bert barked.

"Exactly." She had to remember he was leaving. She had to remember she'd lived these past six years without him and been fine. Maybe not blissfully happy, but fine. When he left, she'd be fine again. "It's probably best if we don't see each other. It would only complicate things."

She parked in front of her family home, opened the back door for the dogs, then went around to the hatchback so she could collect the pups in the kennel she'd borrowed from the clinic. "What's all the ruckus?" She lifted them up high enough to see them. "You can't be hungry already. And you can stop singing because the song is over." She pulled out the playpen Jenna had offered her and closed the hatch.

She turned to see Sterling's truck turn down the drive and slow to a stop.

He turned off the truck and climbed down. He wore a dark brown cowboy hat and jeans that had her propping herself against her car. He stopped long enough to give the dogs a gruff rubdown, then headed straight to her.

"What are you doing—"

His lips found hers before he'd wrapped her up in the warmth of his arms. Firm and gentle and long enough to have her swaying into him. With a groan, he lifted his head. "That. Kissing you."

She blinked. He'd followed her for a kiss? She was equal parts giddy and frustrated. Was he planning on doing that again or climbing back into his truck and driving off?

"Do I need to worry about Buzz coming out here?" He kept right on holding her. If anything, he was pulling her more firmly against him.

She shook her head. "Is that really why you followed me?"

"It's a pretty damn good reason." His gaze swept over her. "Plus, I've missed the dogs."

She smiled. "I'm sure they've missed you, too. Since you're the one always sneaking them food."

"Only once or twice." He smoothed her hair back, his fingers caressing each curl.

"A day." With a single look, he had her off-kilter. "Are you…? Was this a drive-by sort of thing or do you plan on staying awhile?" His smile had her leaning more heavily against him.

"I'll take that as an invitation. As long as you don't have plans."

If he was being playful. She would, too. "I do. I have a date in about an hour." The puppies would be starving by then.

His arms slipped free. "Oh?"

"A dinner thing." She shrugged, surprised by his reaction. "But you can come, if you want." She waited for him to catch on.

"On your date?" He wasn't happy. "I'll pass." He reached for the collapsed playpen. "I'll help you set up and go."

Her attempt at teasing was turning into an epic failure. He was mad and, from the looks of it, getting madder. She led the way, unlocking her door and pushing it wide.

"Is your date with anyone I know? Dean, maybe?" He unzipped the playpen cover and immediately went to work putting it together. His tone was brittle and his gaze was full of judgment.

Dean? Really? Why was he acting this way? "I don't know their names."

"Their?" He stood and ran a hand along the back of his neck.

"Sterling, I was trying to be funny." She lifted the kennel, pointing at the puppies. "My dinner *dates*. No names." She stared into the kennel. "I guess I need to work on my delivery, huh, guys?"

He cocked an eyebrow at her. "Ha-ha."

"Why would it bother you, anyway? I haven't

heard a peep from you since you dropped me at Buzz and Jenna's." As soon as she'd said it, she saw her mistake.

His grin was devastating. "And you missed me." He stepped forward to take the kennel from her hand and put it on the floor.

"I did not say that." But she couldn't resist leaning into the hand he pressed against her cheek.

"I missed the dogs." He rested his forehead against hers. "And the puppies." He tilted her head back. "But I missed you something fierce."

This was what she couldn't do. When it came to Sterling, she was weak. One touch, one look, and she gave in to him. But, in the end, she'd only wind up hurting herself. She stepped away from him, keeping her tone as light as possible. "You know, our arrangement was for the cabin. We're back in the real world, you'll be leaving soon, so we should stop all the kissing and sweet talk." She glanced at him, noting the rigid set of his jaw.

"If that's what you want—"

"It is." *No, it's not.* She wanted him to touch her, to look at her with fire in his eyes and to tell her how much he loved her. "Don't get me wrong, I had an amazing time, but we both knew it was temporary." She forced a smile. "I don't want things to get complicated. I'm sure you don't either."

He wasn't smiling. "Having a baby will complicate things."

"We don't know if that's happening." She tugged the hem of her red sweater down. "And if I am…pregnant, we'll figure out how to co-parent without sacrificing our own happiness." People did it all the time and they looked happy.

His dark gaze fixed on her face, but he didn't say anything for a long time. Even the puppies went quiet, as if they were waiting to hear what he had to say. "This good?" His hand rested on the playpen.

That's it? No argument? She should be relieved, but she wasn't. "It is." She nodded. "But I was planning on putting it in the bedroom. Sorry."

"For what? It makes sense. I didn't ask where you wanted it." He collapsed the playpen. "This way?"

"Yes." She carried the kennel into her room and placed it on the bed, then flipped on the overhead lights. "I was thinking there? At the foot of the bed?"

While he set up the playpen, she went out in the hall to dig through the linen closet for the blankets and towels rarely used. She came back to find Bert, Ernie and Sterling sitting on her bed beside the howling kennel.

"It sounds like they're starving to death." When

Sterling stood and helped her spread out the blankets in the bottom of the playpen, Cassie did her best not to stare at his impressive, jean-clad ass.

"They ate less than an hour ago. Bert and Ernie were singing Christmas carols and these two joined in. I guess they're not done singing?" She opened the kennel and lifted a pup. "Go see Sterling."

"Their eyes are open." He rubbed the puppy's head. "What's the hold up with names?"

"I'm calling them Big and Little, but…" She shrugged and pulled the other pup from the kennel. "Nothing seems to fit." She held the puppy close. "Frannie suggested Peanut and Butter. Garrett didn't approve. He didn't like Monica's idea either. Harry and Styles." She placed the puppy in the playpen.

"What did Garrett want?" He put his puppy next to hers, watching as the two of them grunted and wriggled around and over each other.

"Gregor and Mendel. A mathematician. But Garrett wasn't one hundred percent and said he had to think it over because names were important." She sat on the bed. "I can't say I disagree with him."

Sterling sat beside her, absentmindedly scratching behind Bert's ear. "The place is yours now?"

"Sort of. Mom and Dad love Florida but stay

here when they come to visit. It's too small for Buzz and Jenna and their crew, so they have a place in town. Close to work and school—which makes it easier with all the kids."

"What about all the animals? When I was here last, there was the makings of a zoo."

"Buzz. He never found an animal he could bear to part with." She yawned. "But Jenna and the kids shifted his priorities a bit. He found homes for all of them at a couple of local wildlife refuges. The Mitchells bought our cattle. Angus is letting me board our horses at his ranch, for now. A lot of our fences need repair and a spring storm took off part of the barn roof, so the horses are better off on the McCarrick Ranch." The slight dip in his nose made her ask, "Have you talked to them? The McCarrick brothers?" His escort out of town. She was going to let them have it when she saw them next.

"I did. They had some damage to their place, so I helped out a bit, and we hammered out the details for an official contract." He looked at her. "You were right about clearing the air. It's good to know where we stand and agree on expectations."

"I'm so glad." She smiled. "I think it'll be a win-win for both of you."

He swallowed hard, his gaze holding hers. "Here's hoping." Ernie was trying to nose his way under Sterling's arm, so Sterling lifted it long enough for the dog to cuddle up and rest his head in Sterling's lap. "The cabin's been awful quiet since you all left. Feels colder, too. Marvin stopped by the other morning. We had coffee together."

"I like him. I think he'll find friends here. I hope he does. Maybe you can coax him into coming to the Christmas parade?" She nibbled on the inside of her lip. "If you're still here, of course."

"My plans haven't changed. I'm staying through the holidays, at least." He stared out the large picture window. "But I'm heading out tomorrow—for a quick overnight." His sigh was resolved. "I wanted to let you know. In case you did finally start missing me." There was that grin again.

She drew in a steadying breath. A man shouldn't be this good-looking. It was too distracting. But his grin was fading and his gaze drifted back to the window. "For work? Everything okay?" She studied his profile, the brackets around his eyes and the thin line of his lips.

"My father." He started to reach for her hand but stopped. "He sounded poorly when we talked last. I feel like I should go see him."

She took his hand. "Then, go."

"It'd be easier if he wasn't such a pain in my ass. The man is meaner than a snake." His voice was gruff and his grip on her hand tightened. "His assisted living facility, Shady Oaks, is in Hobart, Oklahoma. I figure since I'm close, I should swing by and wish him a merry Christmas."

The man had inflicted so much pain on his son, he didn't deserve Sterling's time or love. It wasn't fair. The idea of Sterling throwing himself into the line of fire left a knot in her stomach. But Sterling was going anyway. Her heart thudded.

"He won't thank me for it, but it's the decent thing to do."

She squeezed his hand, letting him talk.

"I know he's not much of a father, but he is my father. I can't turn my back on him—even if he's done the same countless times to me."

"You're the better man, Sterling. A good man." *The man I love.*

He shrugged and glanced at her stomach. "If I am, I have him to thank for it. In a way, he showed me what not to do. How not to treat someone you love—how not to be a husband or father." He gave her hand a final squeeze. "I'll be back and stay until we know." He stood, patting Ernie and staring down at her. "You take care of yourself. You boys, take care of your momma." He seemed to hesitate, as if he had something more to say, then changed his mind. "I'm going to pack up and head out in the morning."

"Be careful driving." She longed to grab his hand. "Your father might not appreciate the visit, but I'm proud of you for taking the high road. I imagine it's no easy thing."

The corner of his mouth ticked up. "That's nice to hear. It means a lot, coming from you."

Long after the front door closed and the rumble of Sterling's truck had faded into the distance, regret had her stomach churning. Instead of offering him the support and comfort he needed, she'd pushed him away. He shouldn't have to face his father alone. He shouldn't have to make the drive back without someone to talk to. She stood and headed for the kitchen to use the landline telephone. "Jenna? It's Cassie. I need a huge favor."

Sterling parked in the Shady Oaks lot and stared at the brick structure. Wreaths hung from the front columns. Green-and-red lights shone from each window. Large potted poinsettias sat beside the front doors. The lawn was dusted with snow, and several holiday inflatables bounced in the steady Oklahoma breeze. From outside, it looked almost cheerful.

He'd brought his father a fast-food hamburger, new slippers and a bag of cinnamon candy. His father would either eat the burger or throw it at him. The only way to find out which was to go inside. He ran a hand over his face, blew out a slow breath, grabbed the bags and opened the truck door. The air was icy, so he tugged his jacket closed and held on to his hat as he hurried across the parking lot.

"Look who the wind blew in." The receptionist gave him a quick hug and had him sign in. "He's in a mood."

"Nothing new." Sterling winked and headed down the hallway to room 310. He took another deep breath and knocked.

"What?" his father wheezed

Sterling stepped inside. "Just me." He paused long enough to take in the change in his father. "Got you hooked up?"

His father waved a hand at him. "They say I need it." He pulled the cannula from his nose. "It tugs on my ears."

The monitor next to his father's bed started pinging. His oxygen levels were steadily dropping. "I think you need that, Dad."

"Now you're a doctor, too?" He held the cannula in his hands. "What's that?" He eyed the bags.

"You said you were hungry." He handed over the bag of food. "Double bacon. Large fries."

His father nodded. "Sounds edible."

The monitor was beeping more rapidly, but his father ignored it.

"Mr. Ford." A tall woman came into the room, her expression stern. "You have to keep that on your face. You know that. Your lungs aren't moving enough air without it." She smiled at Sterling.

"I don't like it," his father snapped.

"I imagine you'd like a full-face mask even less. It'll cover your whole face and it's pretty powerful. Doc has a note for it if you don't keep your cannula on." She waited, her hands on her hips.

He glared at the woman but put the cannula back on.

"Thank you, Mr. Ford. What did you get?" She leaned forward. "That looks delicious."

"And I ain't sharing." His father held the bag away from her.

"I don't blame you." The woman winked at Sterling. "Are you the son? My name is Betty. I'm on your father's care team."

"I don't envy you that job." He shook the woman's hand. "It's nice to meet you."

She laughed. "Oh, I can be just as sassy as he is, don't you worry. And he goes on and on about you. How proud of you he is."

Sterling's expression must have surprised her.

"My grandpa was the same. Never said a kind word about me to my face but did nothing but sing my praises to any and every person he talked to." She shook her head. "Don't get me started. Stubborn old coots, the both of them."

Sterling was too dumbfounded to respond.

"You have a nice visit." She leaned around Sterling. "You keep that mask on for me, Mr. Ford. Please."

His father nodded, eating his French fries one at a time.

"She seems nice." Sterling pulled a chair up to sit by the bed.

His father ate another fry from the bag. "She's never given you a sponge bath."

Sterling laughed, hard.

"You still in Granite Falls?" His father took the burger from the bag and unwrapped it. "Get any work done?"

"I did. Negotiated them down and locked them in to favorable terms." He sat back. "They know their horses."

His father grunted and took a huge bite of burger.

Sterling sat quietly, looking around the sand-colored walls with interest. His father wasn't the sentimental type, so most of what had been tacked up were jokes, faded pictures of people Sterling didn't know, newspaper clippings and a photo of Sterling, shaking hands with the president of the National Rodeo Company after his promotion. He glanced at his father, who had his head back on the pillows as he chewed very slowly.

"You good?" Sterling noticed the tremor in his father's arm.

"Mmm-hmm." He kept chewing.

The bed beside his father was empty. When he was here a few months ago, his father had a roommate. Poor man didn't know who or where he was, but he'd been happy. Always smiling and letting his father choose their television program. His father said when he'd picked something scary, his roommate would pull his curtain around and hide under the covers. His father had thought that was hilarious. Sterling had assured him it wasn't.

His father swallowed, sat still and opened his eyes. "That's a good burger." He lifted his head and started coughing. A lot.

Sterling hopped up and offered his father the ice water.

His father pushed it away, his coughing increasing.

"What can I do?" He couldn't just stand there and watch his father turn purple.

His father shook his head, alternating wheezing and coughing.

"You eating too fast?" Betty poked her head in. "You know you have to go slowly. And you need your bed propped up so the food doesn't get stuck." She started to elevate the head of the bed.

"I don't want it up." His father held on to the bedrails.

"It helps when you eat, Mr. Ford." Betty kept elevating the bed.

"I don't give a shit. I'll put it back down the minute you walk out that door." His father slapped the hamburger down on his bedside table and crossed his arms over his chest. "Bossing me around, telling what to do." He yanked the cannula off and scowled at the woman.

"Looks like you're full of energy today." Betty patted his shoulder. "Maybe you wanna go for a ride in your wheelchair? I bet your son could take you out for a stroll around the garden?"

Which sounded like a terrible idea to Sterling.

His father continued scowling her way.

"I'll get your wheelchair." Betty waved. "We'll get you bundled up, too."

It took a good ten minutes to get his father into a sweatshirt and coat. His father complained the whole time, while Betty and a nurse's aide chatted like nothing was out of the ordinary.

"You ready?" Betty stepped back, smiling.

His father continued to glare.

"You two have fun." Betty leaned closer. "He likes being outside."

Sterling wasn't sure he believed it, but he pushed the wheelchair down the hall and out the back doors, into the garden. It was part of patient care. Those who were able helped tend the flowers. Those who weren't would come out and chat with the ones working. At the moment, the garden was empty. A couple of shrubs had candy-colored lights, and a large pine tree on the other side of the fence had been decorated and lit up.

"That's nice." Sterling pushed him along the concrete path to the Christmas tree.

"Kids came over from the school and sang. And did this." He stared up at the tree. "It was horrible. The screeching, some crying. I covered my ears."

Sterling had to swallow another laugh. "I'm sure they meant well."

"I'm sure they were trying to short-out some hearing aids." His father waved them forward. "Over here. You can see the park. It's decorated up nice, but there was no wailing and screeching to suffer through."

Sterling pushed until his father held up his hand. He locked the wheels and sat on the wrought iron bench. "That's a nice view."

The park had plenty of green space. There were different-colored Christmas trees placed all around. The large fountain, in the center of the park, was illuminated with alternating red and green and white lights.

They sat in silence, watching the families and people milling about. Some Frisbee players. Some kids playing hide-and-seek. A woman walking her dogs. A group of teens playing soccer. Wait… He scanned the group again. He knew that woman.

Cassie. Bert and Ernie, too. Was he seeing things? What the hell was she doing here? Hobart wasn't a short drive, yet here she was. Cassie. Seeing her…calmed him. Did she know that? As far as he knew, she didn't have a reason to come to Hobart. But he wasn't going to assume she'd come for him. She'd throw a ball, they'd race to it and whoever got to it first brought it back to her. She laughed when the two of them tried to carry the ball together.

"She's something." His father nodded.

She threw the ball again and the dogs went tearing after it. This time her gaze wandered. He had a pretty good idea what she was looking for, so he stood up and waved. She stood on tiptoes and waved back, calling the dogs over.

"You know her?" His father smoothed his coat.

"I do." He smiled at his father. "And I can't believe she's here."

"Hi." Cassie was winded by the time she reached the fence. "Fancy meeting you here."

"It's a surprise." And Sterling wasn't sure what to make of it. "Cassie, this is my father, Billy Ford. Dad, this is Cassie."

His father stared at her for a long time. "You're prettier than I remembered."

She wasn't pretty. She was beautiful. Sterling still couldn't believe she was here.

"Thank you." Cassie smiled. "It's nice to see you again, Mr. Ford."

Bert and Ernie were whimpering and trying to poke their heads through the fence.

"Hey." Sterling reached through to give them each a pat. "You have to stay on that side. I don't think dogs are allowed."

"Who the hell cares?" His father pointed at the gate. "Open it up and let them in."

Cassie stared up at him, those blue eyes of hers sparkling. "You heard the man."

His father chuckled.

Sterling shook his head and opened the gate. Bert and Ernie came bounding in to sniff and circle his father's wheelchair before sitting, tails wagging, at his father's slipper-encased feet.

"You still got that ball?" his father asked.

Cassie handed it over. "I'll warn you, they never get tired."

His father chuckled. "Well, I do." It didn't take long and his father was wheezing and shivering.

"We better head back inside." Sterling patted his father on the shoulder.

"Of course." Cassie smiled. "Come on, boys. Maybe we can come see you again, Mr. Ford?" She waited, but his father didn't respond. "We'll see them later," she said to the dogs, leading them back through the gate and pulling it closed behind them.

His father was quiet all the way to his room. With his and Betty's help, they stripped off his extra layers and got him into his bed. And still, his father stayed quiet.

"I got you a Christmas present." Sterling placed the bag on his father's bed.

"Why did you bring her here?" His father was staring up at him, so angry he was shaking. "Did you drive all this way to rub my face in it? To show me I was wrong?" He coughed, then went on. "You got the girl and some dogs and a perfect life, and I'm stuck in this pigsty." He wheezed. "She's the reason you're not taking me with you, isn't she?" He coughed again. "You hate me so much you'll pick her over your own father?" He was shaking his head, his hands fisting. "Then, go on, ride off into the sunset and leave me to rot." He picked up the gift bag and heaved it at him. "I won't take a present you bought to ease your guilt." He was coughing so hard he couldn't get any more words out.

All Sterling could do was stare. "You really think that's why I'm here?"

"I know it!" He bellowed, then collapsed against the bed, coughing.

Sterling stepped forward, but his father held his hand out.

"Don't you come near me. I want you gone. You're no son of mine."

Betty came running in, plugging him into the oxygen and clicking some knobs. "He's just tired. He got so excited you visited. He'd been telling us about it for days now."

Sterling shook his head.

"Tell him to go!" His father yelled, pointing his finger at Sterling. "Make him leave. He's not my kin. This is my room. I want him outta here."

Betty's smile vanished.

"It's fine." Sterling picked the gift bag up off the floor. "I'll check in at New Years, Dad." He walked out of the room before his father could say another word. "He might want this later." He set the gift bag on the receptionist's counter and walked out the front door.

Cassie was waiting for him on the bench out front. She was talking to the dogs but jumped up the minute she saw him. "Sterling?"

He shook his head, more numb than anything.

Cassie stood on tiptoe and wrapped her arms around his neck. He pulled her against him until his father's red face and hateful words faded. All that remained was Cassie. He took a deep breath and rested his hand against her back, just taking her in. Her scent. Her breath against his cheek. The caress of her fingers through his hair. She covered him in warmth so soothing he melted into her.

"Thank you." He whispered against her neck.

"Let's go." She tugged him along. "I called in a few favors and left the puppies with Jenna and was dropped off here so I could ride back with you. The boys, too. I hope that's no trouble." She glanced back over her shoulder, her eyes so blue.

He tried to smile. "You're nothing but trouble." He gave her hand a squeeze. "But I wouldn't have it any other way."

Chapter Thirteen

Cassie took over driving when they stopped for gas and snacks at the halfway point. Whatever happened with his father had left Sterling wound up and quiet. She didn't push conversation on him or ask him any questions. She hadn't come to entertain him, she'd come to be here for him—whatever that meant.

An hour outside Granite Falls, Sterling dozed off. He'd snore softly, jerk awake, then ease back to sleep. Poor Sterling. Even in sleep, he was tormented.

They were a few miles from her house when heavy snowflakes started to fall. "Really?" she murmured, turning on the windshield wipers.

"What?" Sterling asked, wiping his eyes. "Is it snowing?"

"It can't be. We are in Texas, aren't we?" She scanned radio until they found a weather update. Snow only. No ice or rain. "I guess that's not so bad."

He nodded but didn't comment.

She turned off the radio and hummed "Santa Claus is Coming to Town" softly. When she finished, she moved on to "Hark! The Herald Angels Sing." She was halfway through "Deck the Halls" when she turned onto the gravel drive and parked in front of her house.

"You're not going to finish?" Sterling asked. "If you don't, that song will be stuck in my head for hours."

"Really?" She turned to find him watching her and smiled. "Maybe, later." She parked the truck, swinging the keys around her finger. "Coming in?"

He shook his head.

"This time, it is an actual invitation. Please come inside." She opened the truck door. "Come on, boys." She motioned for him to follow and hurried to the front door.

"I need my keys, Cassie."

She heard his door slam and slipped inside. He'd had a hell of a bad day. The way he'd clung to her in the parking lot had told her all she needed to know. He'd been shaken and he didn't need to be alone.

He propped his hands on opposite sides of the doorframe. "Keys, please."

"You'll have to find them." And she sprinted from the room. He was in a dark place and might not be thinking straight. She didn't want him turning to alcohol when he could turn to her. He'd worked too hard. She couldn't stand by and see that work undone. She shoved the keys into her underwear drawer and covered them, then went around the room, opening and closing things—to throw him off.

The front door closed, and Bert and Ernie barked.

"Sterling?" She frowned, nervous and flustered. "Sterling?" She peered into the hallway. No Sterling. Did he have an extra set of keys? She ran down the hall—to find Sterling slumped forward on the couch. "Oh, thank goodness." She pressed a hand to her chest.

He scratched at the stubble on his jaw. "Is there a reason you're hiding my keys?"

"I… I want to make sure you're okay." She sat on the other end of the couch. "I know you're upset—"

"I'm tired, Cassie. Worn out." He glanced at her. "I need sleep."

"I don't think you should drive home." She was nibbling on the inside of her lip. "I'm worried about you."

"It's not far." He nodded, his gaze slipping to her mouth.

"I know but… You can sleep here." She smiled at him, pleading, "I'd feel better, Sterling. If you're okay with it?"

"I'm okay with it." He sprawled on the couch, draping a hand over his eyes.

"You don't look comfortable." His feet hung off the end and she knew there was a spring poking through one of the cushions.

"I am." He grumbled, turning onto his side to face away from her.

"Are you mad at me?" she whispered.

He sighed. "A little."

"Why?" she whispered again.

He sat up and rested his knees on his elbows. "Tell me where to sleep." His dark eyes settled on her face.

She frowned. "You are mad at me."

He stood, rolling his head. "I'm not mad at you, I'm mad at the situation. There are things I want to say that I can't. Things I want to do that I can't." He turned to look at her. "I wish we were still stuck in the damn cabin so I could touch you."

Her heart slammed against her chest. "Me, too."

He took a step closer. "What does that mean, exactly?"

"It means you're going to sleep with me." She stood and held her hand out.

"I'm serious about sleep. I've no plans to seduce you." He took her hand.

"I know." She nodded, leading him down the hall. "Go take a hot shower, you'll feel better." She opened the linen cabinet, handed him a towel and pushed him toward the bathroom.

He might not have any intention of seducing

her, but she wasn't averse to the idea of seducing him. Alongside her hard caramel candies, a bag of dog treats and some sodas, she'd purchased a big box of condoms. She'd shower and shave and rock his world.

He emerged with a towel wrapped around his waist. His eyelids drooped and his too-long hair was a floppy mess.

"You're asleep on your feet." She handed him the pants he'd let her borrow. "They're clean. Go to bed. I'll be quiet."

He took the pants and she went into the bathroom.

She turned on the shower and started humming "Here Comes Santa Claus." Rose-scented shaving gel. A new razor. A loofah. All the tools to groom and beautify—and make her smell irresistible. She hummed her way through her leg shaving, slathered herself up with the rose oil and buffed her shoulders and toes and everything in between.

She brushed her teeth twice, wrapped herself in a towel and tiptoed from the bathroom to her bedroom.

Sterling was snoring against the pillows. No twitching. No movement. He was sleeping hard.

Bert and Ernie lay in their usual spots at the foot of the bed, sleepy-eyed and content as she flipped off the lights and slid in beside Sterling.

Her brain wouldn't turn off. Her parents were

coming in a few days and would stay through the holidays, so she needed to stock the pantry and air out their room. She shopped for presents throughout the year, so that was covered. All that was left to do was the wrapping.

She began a mental grocery list, working through their traditional Christmas dinner and the treats they made together.

If she went shopping tomorrow, she'd go ahead and get a pregnancy test. It was still early, but she'd rather be prepared. Plus, she'd rather keep her predicament to herself and buying one with her mother in tow wasn't exactly ideal circumstances. She and Sterling needed to talk it all out before anyone else found out. It was their business.

It'll be okay. His words.

"You're way over there." Sterling's voice was gruff. He slid an arm beneath her and pulled her against his side—and groaned. "You're missing part of your outfit."

"I'm missing all of my outfit." She rested her head against his chest. "Go back to sleep," she whispered.

He chuckled. "I'm tired. I'm not dead." He rolled over her, his lips catching hers. They were tender kisses. Sweet and slow. His hands were just as tender. His fingers traced along every dip and curve and his lips trailed after.

He kissed his way down her side to her hip. "No condoms."

She shook her head, panting. "Wrong." She slid out of bed, ran down the hall and ran back with the box. "Ta-da." The astonished smile on his face made her embarrassment over buying a box of condoms in a crowded convenience store worth it.

"You were thinking ahead." He took the box. "I think this is my favorite surprise ever." He ripped open the box and tugged her back onto the bed. He made use of his hands and mouth in a way that had Cassie coming apart before he slipped a condom on and made them both climax this time.

She was breathing heavy, tingling all over, and delightfully worn out. "That was... That was... Wow."

"Now I can sleep." He chuckled and pulled her against him, her back to his front, and wrapped an arm around her. "You being there today meant a lot. I'm glad he wasn't mean to you—"

"But he was mean to you, wasn't he?" She hugged his arm close and burrowed closer to him. "And that's not okay."

"I'm used to it. Today showed me that I'll never understand how he thinks or why he's so quick to think the worst. Honestly, it makes me sad that he's so hell bent on being mean and miserable." He pressed a kiss to her temple. "How I react to him is up to me." He nuzzled the back of her.

"I'm sorry," she whispered.

"Other than hiding my keys, you've got nothing to apologize for." He nipped at her earlobe.

"I'm not sorry for that." She smiled into the dark. "If I hadn't, you'd be gone and you wouldn't have done all the amazing things you just did to me."

He chuckled.

"Your keys are in the top-left drawer." She murmured, feeling comfortably sleepy.

"Are you kicking me out?"

"No. I'm leaving the choice up to you. I feel bad forcing you to stay." Her hand tightened on his arm and she burrowed closer. "If you want to go, you can. I'd rather you stayed." She yawned.

He tugged the blankets up and tucked them close. His arms anchored her against him. She could get used to drifting off to sleep in his arms.

"Cassie?" he whispered. "Don't hate me. Please, don't hate me."

She could hear him, but she wasn't sure if it was him or if she was dreaming. Why would she hate him for that...? Had something happened? What had he done? No. She must be dreaming. There was no way she could ever hate Sterling when she was awake. She loved him too much.

Sterling watched as Angus rode a pretty paint horse around the arena. "How old?"

"Eight." Angus brought the horse to a stop. "She's a sweet temperament."

Sterling nodded. He could see it in her eyes. Smart, too.

"I'd hate to part with her." Angus tipped his black felt cowboy hat forward.

"Meaning you're going to make me pay top dollar?" Sterling grinned. "We'll talk." He swung down from the pipe fence. "Something tells me that paint isn't the only reason you called me out here."

"It is." Angus nodded. "And it's not." He glanced Sterling's way. "It'd be a coup if you rode with us in the parade. Give us bragging rights and all."

"I don't know about that, but I'll ride." Sterling slanted his hat to keep the sun from his eyes.

"Well, it's not just the parade. The news and radio people will be there—talking about how the town's pulled together and all that. Dougal and I figure we can slip in there, get some free advertising. Doing business with the National Rodeo Company will help our ranch, no doubt about it."

Sterling could appreciate that. Marketing cost a pretty penny. If they could get some for free, why the hell not. "I'll be there."

"You can ride the paint. See for yourself what a prize she is." Angus clapped him on the shoulder.

Sterling eyed the horse again. He could think

of a few private buyers who might be interested. He'd make some calls and see what he could come up with. "You'll deliver her?"

"Of course." Angus waved him away, his eyes narrowing as he stared down the road to their ranch. "Looks like Buzz. He brings the kids out to see the horses now and then." He shot a concerned look Sterling's way. "Is it going to be a problem?"

"For me? No." He draped his arms over the metal fence, content to stay out of the way.

Angus nodded and headed toward the main barn.

Sterling glanced in the direction of the red minivan and the stream of children pouring out of it. Buzz came around to give Angus a handshake and the whole crew headed for the barn.

Sterling was torn. He'd like to think that he and Buzz had settled all that needed settling last time they'd spoken. There was a chance Buzz'd gone along with it all because Cassie and Jenna both expected it. If he was going to pursue Cassie, he didn't want Buzz to stand in the way.

If? He chuckled and pushed off the fence. There was no *if*. She was his. She always had been. She might be holding back but… Her showing up at Shady Oaks had given him hope he'd never dared to have before. She'd come all that way for him. She had to love him. At least, he hoped like hell she did.

He was almost to his truck when Buzz flagged him down.

The moment of truth.

"Buzz." He held his hand out.

"Sterling." Buzz's grip wasn't exactly welcoming. "I figure we should clear the air."

"Fine by me." He shoved his hands into his pockets and hoped clearing the air meant talk—not fight.

Buzz glanced over his shoulder at the barn. "Jenna thinks there's something going on with you and Cassie. I'd like to think she's wrong—"

"She's not." Sterling wasn't playing games. "You asked a direct question, so I'm giving you a direct answer. I love her. I always have. She doesn't know that yet, but I'm hoping she'll hear me out."

Buzz stared at him.

"A man can change, Buzz. If I could go back and knock some sense into the boy that hurt her, I would. In a heartbeat. But I can't. And that confused boy? That's not who I am now. I know what matters. For me, that's pretty much all Cassie."

"I'm just supposed to believe that?"

"No offense, Buzz, but what you choose to believe is your decision. The only one that needs to believe me is Cassie." He saw the little girl peeking around a bale of hay. "You sneaking up on us?"

The little girl smiled and ran to Buzz.

"Monica said you having a gwown-up talk and you might punch each othew's faces." Frannie shook her head. "But you won't do that. Jenna would be sad. Aunt Cassie would be, too, because she likes you the way Jenna likes Buzz."

Sterling chuckled. "Is that so?"

Frannie nodded. "Yep."

Buzz sighed and stared up at the sky overhead. "Frannie, who told you that?"

"Jenna." She smiled. "And Jenna is always wight."

"That's a relief. Thank you, Frannie." Sterling winked at the little girl.

Buzz shook his head. "You're done looking at the horses?"

"Nope." Frannie took his hand. "Come see, come see, Buzz."

"I'm coming." Buzz stopped long enough to whisper, "You hurt her and—"

"I know." He frowned at Buzz. "I appreciate you protecting her. I'll protect her, too. And whatever or whoever she wants, I want her to have it. Even if it's not with me, I want her happy."

Buzz nodded slowly. "Then, we both want the same thing."

"Come on, come on." Frannie pulled Buzz by the hand again.

"Lead the way." Buzz let the little girl drag him along.

Sterling ran a finger along the crook in his nose. Considering how it could have gone, he was pleased. Of course, telling Buzz he loved Cassie wouldn't do a damn thing to convince Cassie it was true.

He checked his watch. The Coffee Shop didn't close until two and he had a hankering for a cup of hot chocolate and a gingerbread cookie. He parked and strolled along Main Street, pausing now and then to look in the shop windows. Something sparkled in the antiques-and-resale shop window. Sterling stared at the ring and headed inside.

"Sterling." Dean Hodges nodded his way. "Looking for anything in particular?"

"I wanted to see that ring in the window."

"The wedding set?" Dean's brow furrowed.

Sterling nodded, wishing he'd thought this through. The shop was crowded—next week was Christmas and people were doing their last-minute shopping.

"You want to look at the wedding ring set?" Dean repeated.

"Yes." Sterling pointed. "The set in that window."

Dean took his time finding the key that unlocked the case. When he carried it back to the counter, he looked like he was sucking on a sour lemon. "Here it is."

Sterling studied the bands. One was a circle

of gold and diamonds, the other was a solid-gold band. "I'll take it."

"You don't want to think it over?" Dean eyed the ring. "Women can be picky over their wedding rings."

It was traditional. Not too flashy, but enough to show he valued her. Sterling turned the set slowly. He could imagine it on her finger. "I'm sure." If Cassie didn't like it, he'd get her something else. He hadn't worked out all the details yet, but if he proposed before they knew if she was pregnant, explained that he wanted her either way, she'd see that he really, truly loved her.

Dean slid the hand-written price tag to Sterling and Sterling slid back his credit card. Five minutes later, he was walking to The Coffee Shop with the rings in his pocket.

"Hey, Sterling." Reggie waved at him from behind the counter. "What can I get for you?"

"Hot chocolate and…" He scanned the bakery case. "I'm hoping you have a gingerbread cookie?"

"I do." She nodded. "Coming right up."

He paid and stood at the end of the counter.

"I wanted to say it was really cool, what you did for Cassie." She pushed the money back his way. "She's the one that made me feel welcome in Granite Falls. You know Cassie, she's impossible not to like. She's the best friend I have here and if anything had happened..." She shuddered. "Thank you."

"No thanks needed." He pushed the money back toward her. "I'm thinking the storm hit everyone pretty hard." He paused then. "You have a snowflake cookie and a Santa cookie?"

She nodded.

"Can I take one of each, to go?" He paused. "And where do they sell lipstick? Lots of colors?"

Reggie gave him an odd look. "It sounds like you're putting together a present. For a specific someone? Someone special?"

He nodded.

"I can help." She pulled out a slip of paper and jotted some notes. "I starred her favorite shops."

"I appreciate it." He tucked the paper into his pocket.

"Good luck." Reggie waved as he left.

"Thank you." He had a feeling he was going to need it.

Chapter Fourteen

Cassie stared at the pregnancy test. This was the first time she'd managed to find some time alone. First, her parents' flight had been cancelled due to winter storms, then one of the puppies didn't want to eat and there was an emergency at the vet clinic—which meant she'd had to man the front desk and phones. As soon as closing time hit, everyone had headed downtown to help with the final preparations for the parade. Tomorrow, Christmas would arrive in Granite Falls and the one-week countdown to Christmas would begin.

But first, Cassie needed to see if there would be another arrival in Granite Falls.

According to the test, she should see results in ten minutes. She'd spent eight minutes getting the puppies settled into a kennel until she was done helping with the parade preparations downtown. Bert and Ernie had free run of the place as well as a comfy bed to sleep on. It kept her busy, but she knew how momentous this was. If she was pregnant, everything would change. If she wasn't and she didn't tell Sterling how she felt about him, nothing would change. But if she wasn't and she got up the nerve to tell him? She didn't know what her future would look like.

Eight minutes. Only eight minutes. Was this the result or did she need to wait the full ten minutes for the test to be accurate? Would the tiny blue plus turn into a tiny blue minus? She scanned the directions.

Wait at least seven minutes to read the results.

She stared at the test. At the bright blue plus.

She took a breath and consulted the directions. Typically, a plus sign meant positive. But maybe it meant something different for a pregnancy test.

Nope. It meant the same thing. Plus. For positive. Pregnant.

She stared at her reflection, tugging up her pink sweatshirt to stare at her tummy. Was there really a tiny person in there? A person she and Sterling had made.

Sterling had said it would be okay. She hoped he meant it. She picked up the test and slipped it back inside the box it had come in. Then stopped. She pulled out the second test and repeated the procedure.

The first test could be wrong. It could be.

She paced the lobby of the clinic, watching as the bundled-up citizens of Granite Falls made their way to the park to help set up for tomorrow night's parade. Her whole life was here. Friends and family... And now she'd raise her baby here. With Sterling. It wouldn't be easy, but she believed they could make it work. She nibbled on the inside of her lip, nauseated for the first time. She loved him. So much. Should she start with that? Or would that lead to an obligatory proposal not a love proposal?

She fed the to-be-shredded files through the shredder, then went back to pacing.

When the timer on her phone started chiming, she sprinted for the bathroom.

"Okay." She took a deep breath. "Maybe the package is defective." She slid the second positive test into the box and braced herself on the side of the sink.

It will be okay.

Right. Yes. Sure. It would be. She added a dab of Christmas-holly-red lipstick to her lips and gave her reflection a thumbs-up. With the box in her bag, she did a quick check on the puppies and closed up shop. It was colder than she'd expected, so she pulled her gloves out of her coat pockets and tugged them on.

She walked along, watching the timed lights click on in each and every one of the shop windows as a light snow began to fall. From sparkling snowflake cutouts to a Santa's workshop made out of gingerbread, each shop had their own theme.

It would be even more magical with a baby. "I bet you'll love this time of year just as much as I do." All the wonder and delight brand new and shiny.

She rounded the corner to the park, waving at Mrs. Hodges, Reggie, Skyler and Kyle, and… "Mr. Green?" She was so delighted, she hugged him. "I'm so glad you came."

"Marvin, please. Sterling offered me a ride. And you were the one that told me not to miss the parade, but I figured I should help get things ready, too." He tucked her arm through his. "You were right about meeting people. I get the feeling Penny Hodges is checking me out."

Cassie giggled. "Really? She's actually very nice. She makes treats for Bert and Ernie. And she's a speed walker. Every morning, you'll see her sailing by."

Marvin seemed to consider this. "Does she fish?"

Cassie blinked. "I have no idea. But I can find out."

"Fishing is a must." He patted her hand.

"A real deal breaker, eh?" From the corner of her eye, she saw Jenna's youngest sister, Biddy, toddling after Buzz. Buzz scooped her up and tossed her high, making the baby giggle. It was so precious…

Skyler waved. "You're here."

"I had to make sure the puppies were okay." She smiled. "Have you met Mr. Marvin Green?"

"Nice to meet you." Skylar gave his hand a hearty shake. "I think Buzz wanted your help with the clinic float, Cassie."

"Got it." She scanned the crowd, looking for Sterling. Now wasn't the time to say anything—no matter how much she might want to.

As she was crossing the grass to the vet float, the high school band started playing. When she recognized "Here Comes Santa Claus," she clapped her hands and sang along. It was her favorite Christmas carol, after all.

"I figured that would get your attention." Sterling took her hand.

"Sterling?" She stared down at her hand in his—and at the people who were watching. "What are you doing?" She tried to tug her hand away.

"Making a scene." He dropped to his knee.

Wait? No. How did he know? There was no way he could know. She dropped down onto her knees, too, pleading, "But I need to tell you—"

"Cassie, there is nothing you can say that will change what I'm doing." He smiled at her.

"Why are you doing this?" She shook her head.

"Don't. You don't have to. I don't want a loveless marriage. You don't either, I know you don't."

He frowned. "But, Cassie, I know—"

"No. You don't." Didn't he realize that he was trapping himself? How was she supposed to live with herself if that happened? She tugged her hand free and stood. "I... I...feel sick." Everyone was there. Everyone was watching. The band stopped playing and she fought the urge to run. "I'm sorry, Sterling." She shook her head. "This isn't right."

He stood slowly but made no move to stop her when she started walking, briskly, back to the clinic. She ignored Jenna and Buzz and climbed into her car. She'd come back, later. But right now, she needed space.

What was he thinking?

He was being noble. She shook her head, braking as the snowflakes picked up. No, that wasn't it.

He didn't know she was pregnant. There was no need to be noble.

Had Buzz strong-armed him into this? That didn't make sense either. Buzz would be happy to see Sterling's taillights disappear into the distance.

So why...? She pulled off her gloves and wiped at her tears.

Don't hate me. Please, don't hate me.

She stomped on the brakes. Her dream. And... she'd told him she'd hate him if he told her he

loved her... Did that mean...? Maybe it hadn't
been a dream. The only way to know was to ask
Sterling outright. Just the two of them. She turned
around and headed down the highway, passed the
turn-off into town, then took the gravel road that
led to their cabin.

She sat, staring at the blinking Christmas lights
in the window, and took a deep breath. Sterling
wasn't here yet. The enormity of what she'd done
began to sink it. She'd left him standing in the
middle of the field with her closest friends and
family watching. She'd run off without thinking about what sort of aftermath he'd deal with.
Her head drooped forward. *I'm so sorry, Sterling.*
She'd wait for him and hope he'd forgive her for
humiliating him. Worse, for hurting him.

Sterling hadn't lost it yet. Everyone seemed
legitimately sympathetic. He'd taken everyone's
whispers, claps on the back and apologies in
stride. He didn't give a damn about what they
thought. What worried him was Cassie.

"What are you going to do?" Buzz walked with
him to the clinic.

"I'm going to talk to her." He adjusted his cowboy hat to buffet the wind. "This whole public
thing was plain stupid. Jenna and Reggie meant

well, but I should have listened to my gut. The only thing flashy about Cassie is her lipstick."

Buzz chuckled. "She looked like a deer in the headlights. I think she panicked."

"I don't blame her." He followed Buzz inside the clinic, his heart in his throat.

"Cassie?" Buzz called out. He went into the back.

Sterling should have kept this between him and Cassie. Somewhere in the back of his mind, he thought she'd like having her friends and family there when he proposed. Jenna and Reggie swore she would. He hoped her reaction was because of the setup, not the proposal itself. If that was it… If she didn't want him, he'd figure a way to deal with that. But until he found her and talked to her, there was no way of knowing what was going on inside that beautiful head of hers.

Her car wasn't parked out front. The vet clinic hadn't been far enough away for her. "She's not here." Buzz waved him back. "She left the dogs and the puppies."

"That's not like her." She took her boys with her everywhere. *Damn it all.* "I'll take them to her."

Buzz nodded. "I'll help you get them loaded up."

The whole way to her house, Sterling was cussing himself. He'd all but dragged her into the spotlight. It would have felt like he was forcing her hand. He knew how she felt about having her decisions made for her. It pissed her off. He'd done the one thing to make her tailspin and he'd done it publicly. As much as he wanted her to marry him, he'd respect her decision. He'd apologize and tell her as much.

He pulled into her drive. "Dammit." He hit the steering wheel. No car. No lights. "No Cassie."

Bert and Ernie sat up and started barking, and a steady howl emerged from the kennel.

He didn't know where she'd go. Did she have a special place? Or a friend she'd go to? He couldn't call her—as far as he knew she hadn't replaced hers. Reggie and Jenna had made sure everyone special was there tonight, so he called each and every one of them. Their answers were all the same. No Cassie. He spent the next hour driving one way, then turned around and circled back.

It was dark and the puppies' howls had turned to hungry whimpers. He had no choice but to head home and feed them. He'd call Buzz and see if there was any news.

He turned onto the gravel road to his cabin and came to a hard stop when he saw her car parked in front of the cabin. "Sorry, boys." He opened the door. "Come on. Let's go." The dogs bailed out and he grabbed the kennel. He started out running but slowed the closer he got to the door.

He needed to think through what he was going to say. He couldn't afford to screw this up again.

The door opened. "They sound hungry." She stooped to pet Bert, then Ernie. "It's cold."

He followed the dogs inside and closed the door. He set the kennel on the floor, hung up his coat and hat, and cleared his throat.

"Sterling—"

"Cassie, hold up. Please. Tonight was… Well, it didn't go so hot." He shook his head. "We've kept our business to ourselves and tonight I turned it into a public spectacle."

"I need to tell you—"

"That's the thing. If you're trying to tell me whether or not you're pregnant, I don't want to know. Not yet. I want you to know that I love you. I have always loved you—I was just too stupid to say anything. I couldn't believe you'd give me a second look, let alone a second chance. I love you and I want to be with you for the rest of my life." He took a deep breath. "I'd rather you didn't hate me for saying all this."

She blinked and tears slipped down her cheeks.

"You said you didn't want to be in a loveless marriage." It hurt to swallow. "If you don't love me, I'll let you go. But I will always be here for you and our baby."

She kept on crying.

"What did I do?" He couldn't stop himself from reaching for her and pulling her into his arms. "Tell me how to make this better. Do you want me to go?"

"No." Her hands pressed against his back. "No. You can't go. You just said you loved me."

"I do." He tilted her face up. "I love you. And I want you to be happy."

"I am happy," she wailed. "I have never—" she sniffed "—been so h-happy."

He cradled her face. "Cassie. Your tears are killing me here."

She shook her head. "They're happy tears." She smiled. "See, I'm happy." She pointed at her wobbling smile. "I was so afraid I'd lost you. I—I humiliated you when—"

"You think I give a damn about what they think?" He smoothed tears from her cheek. "You. You are the only one that matters."

She smiled, her arms wrapping around his waist. "No, I'm not." She kissed him. "Our baby matters." Her eyes were bright blue.

He stared at her. "Baby?"

"Our baby." She ran her fingers along the side of his face. "Since I didn't get you a Christmas present, I guess this will have to do."

"I don't know which is the greater gift. You or the baby." He rested his hand against her stomach.

"You told me it was going to be all right." Cassie gripped the front of his shirt. "You were right."

"That counts as a Christmas present." He smiled. "Let me hear it one more time."

She rolled her eyes. "You were right."

He rested his forehead against hers and stared into her eyes until all the fear and worry was gone. How he'd earned her love, he didn't know. But he'd work hard to make sure he never lost her.

"I love you," she whispered, her eyes locked with his.

"I love you." He kissed her. "And I do have a Christmas present for you." He led her to the couch. "Hold up. It's in the truck." He ran outside and opened the truck. His hard stop had dumped most everything onto the floor. The gift bag was upside down, but Frannie had helped him pack in enough tissue paper that the contents hadn't moved.

"They were hungry." Cassie nodded at the bottle. "I'll open my present in a minute. As far as I'm concerned, nothing can top this."

Sterling set the bag on the table and fed the larger puppy. "I always get Big."

"You have bigger hands." She shrugged. "He fits."

"Well, he's eating faster, that's for sure." He watched as the pup drained the bottle. "Here I was expecting to have to wait." He set the puppy on the braided rug and grabbed the gift bag.

"He's not done." She cradled the puppy close.

"I've got this." He took the puppy from her.

She took the top wrapped item. "What is this?" She opened it and smiled. "A snowflake and a Santa?" She laughed. "Clever." She reached in to pull out another package. Two puppy collars, one dark blue and one light blue. She held them up and laughed. "Santa and Claws? Perfect." She leaned forward to kiss him.

"You're not done." He nodded at the bag.

She reached inside and dug through the paper until she retrieved a small box.

"Hold up." He wiped off the puppy. "You and Claws go play." He set the puppy down. "Your momma and I need to make it official."

Cassie was crying again. Poor Bert and Ernie were both trying to climb into her lap to comfort her.

"It's okay, boys." He opened the box. "It will be—depending on her answer." He knelt in front of her, taking care not to squish a puppy, and held out the ring. "Will you marry me, Cassie Lafferty?"

She nodded, her smile blinding. "I will."

He slipped the ring on her finger, then placed his hand on her stomach. "Don't you worry about a thing, Little Bit. You've got a momma and daddy that love you."

She covered his hand with hers. "You're going to be the best father."

He took a shaky breath. "I'll do my damndest, I promise you that." He sat on the hearth and pulled her into his lap. "Whatever it takes to make you happy, Cassie. If you're happy, I'm happy."

"You know what would make me very happy right now?" She twined her fingers into his hair. "A kiss."

He kissed her, long and lingering and full of love. "With pleasure." His next kiss was gentle. "I love you."

"I love you, too." She kissed him. "Always and forever."

"Always and forever." He smiled down at her.

"Kiss me again." She whispered.

And he did. Again. And again.

* * * * *

#2947 THE MAVERICK'S CHRISTMAS SECRET
Montana Mavericks: Brothers & Broncos • by Brenda Harlen
Ranch hand Sullivan Grainger came to Bronco to learn the truth about his twin's disappearance. All he's found so far is more questions—and an unexpected friendship with his late brother's sister-in-law, Sadie Chamberlin. The sweet and earnest shopkeeper offers Sullivan a glimpse of how full his life could be, if only he could release the past and embrace Sadie's Christmas spirit!

#2948 STARLIGHT AND THE CHRISTMAS DARE
Welcome to Starlight • by Michelle Major
Madison Mauer is trying to be content with her new life working in a small town bar but is still surprised when her boss-mandated community work leads to some unexpected friendships, including a teenage delinquent. The girl's older brother is another kind of surprise—and they're all in need of some second chances this Christmas!

#2949 THEIR TEXAS CHRISTMAS MATCH
Lockharts Lost & Found • by Cathy Gillen Thacker
A sudden inheritance stipulates commitment-phobes Skye McPherson and Travis Lockhart must marry and live together for a hundred and twenty days. A quick, temporary marriage is clearly the easiest solution. Until Skye discovers she's pregnant with her new husband's baby and Travis starts falling for his short-term wife. With a million reasons to leave, will love win out this Christmas?

#2950 LIGHTS, CAMERA...WEDDING?
Sutter Creek, Montana • by Laurel Greer
Fledgling florist Bea Halloran has banked her business and love life on her upcoming reality TV Christmas wedding. When her fiancé walks out, Bea's best friend, Brody Emerson, steps in as the fake groom, saving her business...and making her feel passion she barely recognizes. And Brody's smoldering glances and knee-weakening kisses might just put their platonic vows to the test...

#2951 EXPECTING HIS HOLIDAY SURPRISE
Gallant Lake Stories • by Jo McNally
Jade is focused on her new bakery and soon, raising her new baby. When Jade's one-night stand, Trent Mitchell, unexpectedly shows up, it's obvious that their chemistry is real. Until Jade's fierce independence clashes with Trent's doubts about fatherhood. Is their magic under the mistletoe strong enough to make them a forever family?

#2952 COUNTERFEIT COURTSHIP
Heart & Soul • by Synithia Williams
When a kiss at a reality TV wedding is caught on camera, there's only one way to save *his* reputation and *her* career. Now paranormal promoter Tyrone Livingston and makeup artist Kiera Fox are officially dating. But can a relationship with an agreed-upon end date turn into a real and lasting love?

HSECNM1022

*Madison Mauer is trying to be content with her new
life working in a small-town bar but is still surprised
when her boss-mandated community work leads to
some unexpected friendships, including a teenage
delinquent. The girl's older brother is another kind
of surprise—and they're all in need of some second
chances this Christmas!*

Read on for a sneak peek at
Starlight and the Christmas Dare,
*the next book in the Welcome to Starlight miniseries
by* USA TODAY *bestselling author Michelle Major!*

"I'm going to call my friend who's a nurse in the morning.
She's not working in that capacity now, but she grew up
in this town. She'll help get you with a good physical
therapist."

The warmth she'd seen in his eyes disappeared, and
she told herself it shouldn't matter. It was better they
remember who they were to each other—people who had
a troubled girl in common but nothing more.

She couldn't allow it to be anything more.

"You need a Christmas tree," he said as she started to
back away.

"I didn't see any decorations in your house."

He nodded. "Yeah, but Stella made me promise I would at least get a tree."

"I'll consider a tree," Madison told him. It felt like a small concession. "Although I'm not much for Christmas spirit."

"That makes two of us."

Once again, she wasn't sure how to feel about having something in common with Chase.

He cleared his throat. "I have more work to do—meetings and deadlines to reschedule. I can make it back to the bedroom."

"I'll see you tomorrow."

"I'll be here." He laughed without humor. "It's not like I can get anywhere else."

"Good night, Chase."

"Good night, Madison," he answered.

The words felt close to a caress, and she hurried to her bedroom before her knees started to melt.

Don't miss
Starlight and the Christmas Dare *by Michelle Major,*
available December 2022 wherever
Harlequin Special Edition books and ebooks are sold.

Harlequin.com

HARLEQUIN
PLUS

Announcing a **BRAND-NEW** multimedia subscription service for romance fans like you!

Read, Watch and Play.

Experience the easiest way to get the romance content you crave.

Start your **FREE 7 DAY TRIAL** at
<u>www.harlequinplus.com/freetrial</u>.